Also by Ron Schwab

Sioux Sunrise
Paint the Hills Red
Ghosts Around the Campfire

The Lockes
Last Will
Medicine Wheel

The Law Wranglers
Deal with the Devil
Mouth of Hell
Dismal Trail

The Coyote Saga
Night of the Coyote
Return of the Coyote

Return of the Coyote

Ron Schwab

Poor Coyote Press
OMAHA, NEBRASKA

Poor Coyote Press
P.O. Box 6105
Omaha, NE 68106
www.poorcoyotepress.com

Publisher's Note: This is a work of fiction. Names, characters, places, and incidents are a product of the author's imagination. Locales and public names are sometimes used for atmospheric purposes. Any resemblance to actual people, living or dead, or to businesses, companies, events, institutions, or locales is completely coincidental.

Ordering Information:
Quantity sales. Special discounts are available on quantity purchases by corporations, associations, and others. For details, contact the "Special Sales Department" at the address above.

Return of the Coyote/ Ron Schwab -- 1st ed.
ISBN 978-1943421206

*In memory of Bennie, my best buddy
and purr-fect writing partner.*

Return of the Coyote

1

ETHAN RAMSEY COULD not believe Skye de-Paul was dead. The news had stunned him and rendered him speechless, and he had excused himself from the wounded Lame Buffalo's side on the pretense he would make a search to determine if there were others he might assist. Now he wandered numbly through the smoldering remains of the village, as the acrid smoke bit his nostrils and burned his eyes. At least the autumn sun had broken through the haze and warmed his back this September morning in the Sioux mountain summer village.

Bodies of women and children, including babies, were strewn like rag dolls among the rubble. The dead men were mostly old, but the female corpses spanned the generations. Lame Buffalo had told him that mostly the older girls and young women had been singled out for the rapes. Some had been spared a grisly death, mostly some of the elderly, with a smattering of children and a few younger women who had probably led them into hiding when the raiders struck at dawn. They sat in clusters, staring seemingly into emptiness with their vacant eyes. Menacing black vultures were already circling in the azure skies above, and a few of the more daring scavengers had started to feast on the tiny corpse of a bloodied infant, whose head had been smashed by a rifle butt or some other blunt weapon. The hulking birds retreated and fluttered off to another prospective meal at Ethan's approach. Ethan, a lawyer by profession these days, had earlier served as Army Chief of Scouts out of Fort Laramie and had viewed the carnage of such atrocities before—rendered by both Indian and military combatants. Both seemed to be equally adept at war on the defenseless, he thought. This time, the murderers were, Lame Buffalo had told him, a rag-tag mix of whites, several Pawnee, and a few colored men. The latter, the chief had called "buffalo hairs," referring to the kinky hair that had earned the Negro buffalo soldiers their designation by the plains Indians.

Virtually all the braves and warriors had been absent from the village when the raiders struck. Many were out on a pre-winter buffalo hunt, which with the rapid depletion of the Sioux's multipurpose prey, took the hunters many miles from the village. Others had travelled northward along the Powder River to meet up with Cheyenne allies for a council that might bring war with the whites come spring. This, Ethan knew, Lame Buffalo would have opposed vociferously, supporting his Brule Sioux cousin, Spotted Tail, in efforts to keep the peace. Of course, after today's slaughter, the band's chief may be thinking differently.

As Ethan surveyed the village, he wondered what was going to become of the survivors of the raid. There could be no more than thirty. Their food supplies had been obliterated, deliberately it seemed. The hunters might return with meat that would feed the remnants of the band for a time, but the hunting party might not come back for days, and there were bodies to be disposed of in some fashion with few able-bodied souls to help. There was neither time nor workers to build the traditional platforms and few tools with which to dig graves. He must speak with Lame Buffalo about this. And what if the marauders swung back this way?

His presence here was filled with irony, he thought, as his fingers touched the crisp piece of paper in his shirt pocket. Skye dePaul, known to her Brule relatives as Sky-in-the-Morning, had employed him as a lawyer some months back, after the lynching of two innocent Indian boys in Lockwood, Wyoming, where Ethan practiced law when he was not managing his shoe-string ranch operation. Skye, a half-blood Sioux whose father had pioneered Wyoming and Montana as a French trader and merchant in Cheyenne, had been a teacher at the Quaker school near Lockwood. She had come to his office to ask him to represent her cousin, Bear Killer, who had escaped the lynching and, to further complicate matters, was Lame Buffalo's son.

As it turned out, Ethan's scouting skills had been more important than his lawyering. In the end, Bear Killer's innocence—and that of his dead comrade—had been established but not before Skye lost her lower left arm and Ethan fell in love with her. He had nearly proposed marriage before she brusquely cut him short. She had left him a bank draft for three hundred dollars for his fees, however, which she failed to sign before returning to Lame Buffalo's village to recuperate. This he took as an invitation to visit the village to collect her signature and, hopefully, to explore their possibilities for the future. The pressures of the ranch and his law practice, coupled with his uncertainty about his standing with Skye, had caused him to delay the trip into the mountains for several months. And now he had waited a day too long.

Ethan walked deliberately back to Lame Buffalo's tattered tipi, his grief over the report of Skye's death deferred for a few moments by the need for decisions and action. The front of the chief's lodge was ripped away, and only a few skins remained draped on the lodge poles to provide an illusion of privacy. The chief, who had been a vital man, not yet fifty, lay stretched out on a buffalo robe. Blood pumped out of a gaping hole in his chest, sending rivulets of blood down his rib cage, where it pooled along his side. His body had paled noticeably in the half hour Ethan had been absent.

A wizened medicine man, who looked barely strong enough to lift the buffalo horn rattle he held in this trembling hand, chanted some song with a squeaky voice. A young woman, perhaps seventeen or eighteen years of age, knelt beside Lame Buffalo, grasping his hand. Her doeskin dress was half torn away and hung on her shoulders like a Mexican serape, its seams split and revealing the taut bronzed skin the garment once covered. There was no one else to comfort the chief as he approached his final journey, for both of his wives had been killed during the raid, the youngest being raped and mutilated while several marauders held her husband back as he struggled to charge to her defense. After the leader of the renegades had finished his turn at the young woman, he approached the chief and laughed contemptuously before plunging the military sabre into his chest. All this Lame Buffalo had related after Ethan's arrival.

The maiden turned her head when Ethan entered the circle formed by the lodge poles. "You are the Puma," she said softly. "My father told me you were here. I am Otter. I was looking for Hooting Owl when you first came here." She nodded toward the shaman.

Ethan noted her perfect English, but he was more taken aback by her resemblance to Skye. It was mostly the eyes, he decided, dark and constantly alert and searching. Notwithstanding the soot and raw scratches that covered her face, she was more than pretty and appeared undefeated by whatever had happened to her, reminding him again of another woman. "I am no longer the Puma," Ethan said. "I am not an Army Scout."

"My father wishes to speak with you," she said.

Ethan knelt beside the dying chief and saw that the man's eyes had opened and seemed surprisingly clear. "I am here, Chief."

"My spirit is preparing to depart on the journey to my ancestors. Help my people, Puma. The prophecy revealed by the coyote is not dead. You have a destiny with our people waiting to be fulfilled. Listen to the coyote. And trust my daughter and her brother, Bear Killer, when he returns from the hunt. They will never betray you. Sky-in-the-Morning brought us the white man's words and prepared them for the trials of the road to peace."

Lame Buffalo's eyes closed. A few minutes later he sucked in his last feeble breath. The medicine man started chanting some new song with a voice so weak and lifeless, the sound would not have carried beyond the lodge. Otter touched her father's forehead gently and rose from his side. Ethan half expected her to start wailing and cutting her body as some mourning squaws did, but, on the contrary, she appeared stoic and serene. Ethan got up and walked out of the battered tipi with her, leaving the medicine man to his task of launching the chief's spirit on its proper voyage.

He stood by the young woman, wondering what she was thinking and trying to sort out in his own mind where he fit into this disaster. He did not have to wait long.

"We must do something with the bodies," Otter said matter-of-factly.

"Yes. And soon. What do your customs allow?"

"We have no time for customs. Nothing in Lakota heritage requires leaving the bodies as carrion for the vultures and other creatures. There is a dry creek bed that runs past the south side of the village. We can take them there and wrap the bodies in buffalo and deer hides and group them by families and stack them tightly. Then we will roll stones upon them, so they cannot be reached by the scavengers."

It was eerie. This might have been Skye speaking. Decisive. Pragmatic. Analytical. "What you suggest makes sense. I'll check out the creek bed. Are some of your people able to help?"

"Anyone who can walk will help."

"I have one question."

"Yes."

"Where is Skye's body?"

"Sky-in-the-Morning? It is not in the village."

"Then where is it?"

"It was she they came here for. The men found her and were taking her away. Her mother, Singing Lark, tried to stop them and one of the Pawnee cowards struck her with a war axe. Skye broke free and ran to her mother's side, and she was clubbed and then bound and slung over a horse. They took her with them along with at least three other girls my age or a bit younger."

"But your father said Skye was dead."

"He assumed so. Look around you. Is there any reason to think otherwise?"

He suddenly grasped a sliver of hope. Without proof beyond any doubt of Skye's death, he would not accept it as fact. Never. His first instinct was to mount Patch, his Appaloosa gelding, and start tracking her abductors. The trail would not be cold yet. But they would be moving fast, not knowing when the band's warriors might return and follow them.

"Are you going to leave us?" Otter asked.

"How many raiders were there?" She was silent for a few moments. He could almost see her mind taking a count of the men she had seen.

Finally, she spoke. "Fifteen, probably. No more than seventeen."

They would be easy enough to track. But with that many, what would he do if he caught up with them? He guessed he'd figure that out when he found them—if Skye was not already dead. But how could he leave these people in this condition? He felt something tugging at his shirt, and he looked down and his gaze met the dark, sad eyes of a Sioux boy, no more than eight or nine years old. The side of his forehead was swollen and smeared with blood, and he was clad only in a breechclout and filthy deerskin shirt.

"You Puma, yes?" the boy asked.

"Some of your people call me that. But my name is Ethan."

"Puma better." He pointed to his chest. "Me Running Fox. You help us, Puma?"

The boy's eyes won out.

2

THE MASS BURIALS drug on through the afternoon. True to her promise, Otter rallied the entire village to the task. Old men who could barely walk carried small stones to the banks of the dry creek bed, while the women wrapped bodies in the remnants of tipis and buffalo and deer skin robes. Some boys and younger girls emerged from hiding in the surrounding forest as the afternoon wore on and were quickly put to work by Otter, who by default had assumed leadership of the village.

Ethan carried most of the bodies to the bank of the creek, with Running Fox solemnly hoisting a corpse's leg or arm to help. Otter identified Singing Lark, whose body Ethan placed near those of Lame Buffalo and his wives. The boy stuck with Ethan like a bootmaker's glue, but his emaciated appearance belied the boy's actual strength, and he was quick and agile and seemed able to lift twice his weight. As the hours went by, the somber silence of the encampment gave way to a soft murmur of voices as the survivors seemed to emerge from their shock.

As Ethan walked through the village ferreting out the remaining victims, he felt the familiar tugging at his shirt. He turned to find Running Fox pointing to the body of a young woman who was half hidden by a fallen tipi. He veered toward her and saw she clutched a child of no more than two years, whose head had been nearly decapitated, in her arms. Her buckskin skirt had been torn away, and she had obviously been raped before a bullet mercifully burrowed into her temple.

"My mother," Running Fox said. He pointed to the baby. "My brother." He looked up with his dark eyes, which were tearless, but conveyed an emptiness which Ethan knew would haunt him to the end of his days.

"I will take care of them," Ethan said. "Why don't you go help Otter now?"

"No, me take Little Hedgehog. You take mother. She called 'Good Heart.' All love her."

Ethan found himself speechless, a rare problem for a law wrangler, he thought. He tugged a deerskin from the lodge poles and lifted the toddler from his mother's arms, carefully holding the flopping head in place, and then he lay him on the deerskin and wrapped it tightly around the little body, realizing only then that tears were rolling down his cheeks. Making no effort to wipe them away, he lifted the tiny package and placed it in Running Fox's hands. "I will carry your mother. Hold your brother carefully. Do you understand?"

"Me know what to do. Bring mother."

Ethan lifted the woman into his arms effortlessly. No one was pretty in death, but as they walked slowly toward the dry creek bed, he concluded she must have been beautiful in life. Good Heart. Most Sioux names said something about the person, and his anger grew another notch.

Otter met them at the creek. Wrapped corpses already lined the creek bed and another layer had been started. No sooner did Ethan place Good Heart's body on the earth than two younger women began their somber work. Another older woman took the child from Running Fox's arms.

"Running Fox is an orphan now," Otter said. "Like many others. But we will care for him."

"His father?"

"He died a warrior's death when the soldiers attacked a hunting party last spring. The bluecoats thought that the warriors were renegade Cheyenne who had attacked and burned the home of a family of white settlers. To most white eyes there is no distinction between the tribes or bands."

He noted she said this with some contempt. "It's all so senseless, but I was a part of it once. Many warriors are dead because I led the soldiers to them."

"Yes, I know the stories of the Puma who moved silently in the night seeking and finding his prey."

Ethan felt a small hand slip into his own. "I was doing a job. I was good at it but came to hate the work."

"The Great Spirit has other plans for you now."

"A nice thought, but I think we make our own plans."

"My father had the vision about you and Sky-In-The-Morning on the night of the coyote."

"I've heard the story. I would think that all that has happened would convince you that Lame Buffalo got something wrong."

A small voice said, "Me want to know story, Otter. Tell me."

Otter looked at Ethan. "Running Fox wants to hear of the vision. Surely you would not deny him this?"

This girl-woman had too much of her cousin in her. She was too adept at outmaneuvering him. He shrugged. "If you want to, go ahead and tell him."

"My father climbed up the mountain side to seek the Great Spirit's guidance on whether he should trust the Puma with the life of his son. He waited until the stars started to fade from the sky. He feared that the Great Spirit was unable to help him that night and almost gave up his quest for an answer. And then a coyote he-dog called to his mate from the far end of the valley, and after a time of silence, the she-dog answered from somewhere above the entrance of the cave where my father sat. My father said he closed his eyes and the vision came.

"In his dream, my father saw a river, the flat water . . . the Platte, the white man calls it. On one side stood warriors of our village painted for war and armed for battle. On the other were the blue-coated yellowlegs. They, too, were prepared for war. My father raised his arm to signal his warriors to attack, when from among the yellowlegs appeared the Puma. He waded into the shallow flat water and crossed it to where our people waited. Standing before my father, he held out his arm and cut it with a knife. The blood flowed like milk from the tits of a nursing mare, so my father said. And then, as if from nowhere, my cousin, Sky-in-the- Morning, appeared beside the Puma. She took his knife and sliced her own arm and pressed her bleeding flesh to his, and their blood mixed. And when my father looked again across the river, the yellowlegs were turning their horses away from this place that had been chosen for battle. Then the Puma took my cousin's hand and led her to the water, and they walked away to follow his people. My father turned to the Brule and said, 'Return to your lodges; we shall fight the white man no more.'"

The boy's eyes were wide, and for a moment he seemed distracted from his sorrow. "Me no see what this mean. Puma is good man. Yes?"

"My father believed he could be trusted by our people. He also thought Sky-in-the-Morning and the Puma were meant to be together and to lead our people into the ways of the white man's world. The full meaning of such visions cannot always be known until time reveals them, and sometimes the truth is found in mysterious ways."

Ethan decided to bring story time to a close. "We have work to do. It will be dusk soon." He moved toward the dry creek bed, and saw that the last of the bodies had been stacked, those of Good Heart and Little Hedgehog on the top row nearest to where Ethan and Running Fox stood. Otter had hurried further down the creek bank where Lame Buffalo and her mother and his other two wives had been placed. She spoke loudly to the assembled survivors in Sioux, and suddenly their voices filled the air with surprising strength in a song that seemed more of a collective wailing. He assumed it was a death song of some type. This went on for no more than five minutes when the singing abruptly stopped, and Otter issued what was obviously an instruction.

Then the little band began throwing, pushing, and dropping the accumulated rocks onto the layered bodies until a mound of stone rose above the creek banks. Ethan helped Running Fox cover the place where his mother and brother lay. He thought the boy seemed to take some comfort in the labor of dealing with the task at hand, but he could not begin to imagine the depth of the wounds left by such violent loss. When they were finished, darkness was settling in, and Otter joined them as they headed back to the remains of the village. A few feeble campfires had been started and signaled the way.

And then a sound shattered the stillness of the night that sent shivers down Ethan's spine. It was the long, mournful howl of a coyote from the low mountains above the village. And then another. And another. Others yipped and barked like dogs. There must be a large pack of them, he figured. But they picked a damn creepy time to show up.

"They have returned," Otter remarked.

"What do you mean?"

"We have not heard coyotes for months. It is very unusual. There had always been coyotes in the mountains.

They were a part of our lives. The coyote was my father's medicine animal, and it worried him. He said the coyotes left after his vision. That was when you and Sky-in the-Morning came for Bear Killer and took him back to the white man's village to find justice for the crime that was not his."

Ethan did not know how to reply to this, so he said nothing for some time. Finally, when they arrived at the lodge poles that had formed Lame Buffalo's tipi, they stepped into the roofless shelter and sat down, Running Fox inching close to Ethan and pressing his skinny frame against his shoulder. Ethan spoke to Otter. "We have to do something about your people. I don't think they should stay here. What do you have to eat?"

"I think a search of the village will turn up small amounts of dried venison. In the morning, we will begin to clean up the rubble, and the tipis should have some foods secreted away. There are roots of some plants in the forest that are still edible, and a few of the older boys may be able to kill a deer or two. We can feed the people for as long as a week, I would guess. Then it becomes a problem."

He had been pondering the question of caring for the band while they labored at the burials that afternoon.

Now he made his decision. "I want you to bring your people to my ranch."

"You are not serious?"

"I am. My ranch is in a valley east of Lockwood. You would usually move your village to lower ground for the winter. Your people would never survive here when the storms come, especially after this. There are many deer on my ranch, and I will supplement with beef. I think there are people in our town who would help."

"Whites would help us?"

"Some would. Not all. We can get you through the winter until you decide what to do. I know the army is pressing for the bands to go to the reservation. That might be best for some. Others, such as you, might make a place for yourself outside the reservation. Your language skills will be valuable. But whatever happens, you must survive the winter first."

"But our hunters will come back to an empty village."

"They will figure out what happened. And don't tell me they won't find you with the trail we leave behind. Hopefully, they will bring meat with them."

"But we have no horses, and most of these people cannot walk that distance."

"I will leave in the morning to arrange preparations. This Wyoming Territory is rough country. It will take me less than two days to get to Lockwood and a bit more than two to make the trip back with horses and supplies. A day to round up help and horses and make other arrangements. I'll be back in five days, six at the most."

"Many will not like it, but they will come."

"I'm sure you will see to that."

"Me go with you," Running Fox said excitedly.

"No, you must wait here," Ethan said firmly. "When I return, you will go with us."

"Me will go now," the boy insisted.

Ethan sighed, "No, you will slow me down and you should be with your people."

Running Fox did not reply.

That night, the three slept in the circle of the tipi. Otter had found a tattered buffalo robe and settled in on one side. Ethan fetched his bedroll from his horse and rolled it out on the other. When he finally drifted off into a restless sleep, Running Fox was burrowed in the blankets and curled up against his back, sleeping soundly.

Early the next morning Ethan, astride Patch, rode out of the village, and so did Running Fox, perched behind Patch's saddle, his bony arms wrapped as far as they could reach around Ethan's waist and his fingers clutching his new friend's buckskin jacket.

3

FTER TWO DAYS working his way down the rough, sometimes treacherous, trails of the well-named Rocky Mountains, as well as carrying some extra cargo, Patch was showing serious fatigue, Ethan noted. When they broke out of the forested slopes and onto the grassy foothills above Lockwood midmorning, Ethan decided he would swing by Fletcher's Livery, leave the gelding with Enos Fletcher, and rent two horses to complete the short journey out to the Lazy R. Enos was the master of rehabilitating tired horses, and Patch had earned a few days of Enos's tender care.

Running Fox had been quiet and withdrawn during most of their journey down the mountain. The boy had annoyed Ethan slightly when he repeatedly asked, "How much long we be there?" But Ethan finally started answering "more than two hours" and figured out the boy had no concept of what that meant in terms of time and at least deferred his questions for longer periods. He was a hell of a worker. Ethan would grant the boy that. He scurried to do camp chores at night, looking to Patch's watering and staking the animal out on the best grass before gathering an armload of firewood. By sundown Running Fox was rolled up in his buffalo robe and sound asleep within reach of Ethan's own bedroll.

As he reined Patch around the curve on the narrow, dusty wagon trail that merged into Lockwood's main street, he caught sight of Enos Fletcher snoozing in the old rocking chair he kept in front of the livery stable. The grizzled livery owner did not awaken as they approached, and Ethan could hear him snoring. Tobacco drool clung precariously to the corner of his mouth. He guessed Enos was in his mid-seventies now and entitled to an early siesta.

Reining his gelding to a halt five paces in front of the sleeping businessman, Ethan said in a soft voice, "Enos, I've got some paying business for you."

Enos's head popped up, the tobacco paste dropping from his mouth, and his head swiveled from side to side in confusion before his eyes focused on Ethan. Then he grinned a half-toothless smile and lifted himself clumsily out of the chair, groaning and rubbing his lower back as he straightened up. "Well, if it ain't my favorite law wrangler," he said in a gravelly voice. "Ain't seen you for near a week. Didn't miss you none, but I sort of like my daily visit from Patch."

"You like the money you get from looking after Patch, you old fart. I spend my days working to support Fletcher's Livery."

"Worse causes, son, worse causes." He cocked his head to the side and looked past Ethan with a squinted eye. "And you brung a tadpole along. He's an extra two bits if you leave him for the day."

Ethan dismounted and lifted Running Fox off the horse. "Running Fox, this is Enos Fletcher, distinguished proprietor of Fletcher's Livery. Enos, this is my young friend, Running Fox."

Enos extended his rough hand, and Ethan nudged the Sioux boy to put his own hand out. Enos grasped the boy's hand and pumped it enthusiastically.

"Welcome to Lockwood, young man."

The boy looked at Ethan. "What is hands rub mean?"

"That's how white eyes say they are happy to see you and welcome you. They call it a handshake."

The boy shrugged. "Okay." He gave Enos a faint, tentative smile.

"I'd like to have you put up Patch for a few days, Enos. And spoil him a bit. I'm going to call on some folks while I'm in town. I'll be back later to rent a few horses to ride out to the Lazy R. Joe's going to wonder if I'm ever going to be there to help out."

"Got to tell you, Ethan, when you took on Joe Hollings, you won a blue ribbon for cowhands. He don't need you much. That cowpoke's a workin' fool . . . especially since that young lady he was gonna get hitched to took up with the young banker."

"Yes, I'm lucky to have Joe looking after things. And I'm going to make it worth his while to stay on. But right now I've got more urgent things to take care of and I'd welcome your advice."

"My advice, huh?" He looked at Ethan skeptically.

"Yes, you know everybody in this town, and I need to talk to the right people . . . today."

Ethan told Enos about the slaughter at the Sioux village and the abduction of Skye and the other young women. "And I need help to bring the survivors of the raid to my ranch and to look after them over the winter. I want you to tell me who might be friendly to what I'm doing."

Enos reached into his tattered shirt pocket and pulled out a tobacco plug. He bit into it and gnawed off a chunk and then limped back to his rocking chair and plopped down. He seemed to be ruminating on Ethan's query and silently worked his jaw for a spell, before he spat out a string of gooey tobacco. "Well, Mr. Lawyer, I'd say if you bring a whole slew of Injuns to plant themselves on your ranch, you can look to be the least popular feller in Lockwood. Might as well shut up that weasel shop of yours. I'd say you'd have no more than a dozen folks who'd show up for this party your planning."

"And who are the dozen?"

"Start with Will Bridges. Go to the Quaker school. There's three ladies there . . . two of them have farmer husbands. Methodist preacher might help . . . but don't count on much of the flock. He might lean on a few folks. Josh Wilson at the general store and his woman would likely pitch in. Red Horse would help, even if he is Pawnee."

"You're a little short of a dozen."

"There'll be a few surprises. Oh hell, count me in. I'll loan you all the horses I can spare . . . and two wagons, if you can figure out how to get the damn things up there."

The livery owner's offer caught Ethan off guard. Nobody in Lockwood squeezed a nickel tighter than Enos Fletcher. "I appreciate that, Enos. I really do. Now, I'd better go see Will."

"The tadpole can stay here with me till you're done, if he wants. I could use some help lookin' after the horses."

Ethan was doubtful. The boy had clung to him like a wood tick ever since they met up. He bent down and looked Running Fox in the eyes. "What do you say, Running Fox? Would you stay with Enos while I take care of some business around town?"

"You come back?"

"I'll come back as soon as I can."

"Me like this old man. Me stay."

Enos had worked some kind of magic on the boy, but Ethan couldn't figure out how or when it happened.

4

I
F THERE WAS any man Ethan could call best friend in Lockwood, it would be Sheriff Will Bridges. The white-haired, bushy-mustachioed lawman was a formidable presence with his burly physique and height that reached well above Ethan's six feet two. Ethan knew him to be a kind and gentle man, though, unless provoked. He was more a listener than a talker, but when he spoke, thought and common sense usually lay behind his words.

Bridges leaned back in his wood swivel-chair, with his booted feet resting on his scratched and pocked desk, as Ethan explained the plight of Lame Buffalo's band of Sioux. He rubbed his chin thoughtfully as Ethan spoke, his pale-blue eyes intense.

"That's about it, Will. I've invited a band of Sioux to winter at the Lazy R. Enos thinks I'm bringing a lot of trouble to the county. But the ornery old coot's offered to help out."

"Well, you might be bringing some trouble, but a lot of life brings one kind of trouble or another. It's how we deal with it that counts. Of course, you've taken on a bigger chunk of trouble than most. I do think Enos underestimated the number of folks that will pitch in to help. He's kind of a pessimistic old turd sometimes. No, a lot of folks won't like this a damn bit, but there's a healthy minority who will pitch in to make things happen."

"I hope you're right. There's a lot of work to be done."

"I know you want to hit the trail and find Skye, but if we're going to get these people here, you'll have to lead a party back to the village. The Indians would probably be reluctant to come down if you aren't there to reassure them. I'll get a deputy to ride up with you and ask Sarah if she can twist the preacher's arm and rally some Methodists to get some food supplies together for you to take along when you go back to the village. Maybe I can call out the volunteer firemen to come up with some kind of temporary shelters to put up at your place."

"I'd really appreciate that, Will. I knew I could count on you, but I hate dropping all of this in your lap."

"I suggest you talk to the Quakers. They know at least some of the younger people who have boarded at the school. Maybe they could help get arrangements worked out for care and feeding of these people after they get here."

"I'll do that as soon as I leave here. Then I'll swing by the livery and pick up Running Fox and some horses and head out to the ranch and warn Joe of the storm that's coming."

After he left the sheriff's office, Ethan walked briskly to the Pennock School, which was located on the outskirts of town. As he approached, he noted that the place didn't amount to much, essentially a cluster of whitewashed clapboard buildings that included what appeared to be a small school building and two, even smaller, dormitories lined up with three drab-looking cottages. He knew that beyond the houses, the several Quaker families owned small parcels of farm ground on which they raised fruit and vegetables to market directly to locals, as well as to the general store in exchange for beef and other food-stuffs when cash was in short supply.

He didn't see any sign of activity in the compound, so he turned up the rocky path that led to the school. He was uncertain whether he should knock on the door but finally opted to simply ease it open. He stepped quietly into a single room that was furnished with a half dozen small tables each with a single, two-person bench behind.

There were eight students, ranging from ages six to fourteen, he guessed, sitting at the benches. Two of these appeared to be young Sioux girls. He suspected that they and a few ranchers' kids slept in the dormitories.

At the front of the room, next to her own desk, stood a young, flaxen-haired woman who could not have been more than eighteen or nineteen years old, he thought. Her drab, gray dress, with its high neck, could not hide her attractiveness. She looked at him with cobalt-blue eyes that seemed to ask what in blazes he was doing there.

"Ma'am, I'm sorry to intrude. I didn't see anyone else about, and I'm on kind of an important errand."

"Everyone else is out at the hay ground, trying to get the last cutting in before winter. Can I be of help?"

"Well, I hope so. Could we step outside?"

She hesitated, and then admonished the children to keep quiet and stick to their work, before she eased her way between the desks and joined him. They stepped outside and stood facing each other.

"I'm Ethan Ramsey," he said. "I'm a lawyer here in Lockwood."

"I know who you are, Mr. Ramsey. Skye dePaul told me about thee."

"Nothing terrible, I hope."

"Sorry, she spoke to me in confidence." She extended her hand and he took it, mildly surprised at her firm grip. "My name is Rachael Cooper. Skye and I shared a house when she taught here."

He swore he saw traces of a smile on her stern face. He felt she was making a careful appraisal of his character, as he told her of his dilemma, and she was obviously distraught over Skye's abduction.

"About Skye, do you think she's alive?"

"I have no way of knowing, but I will find out. As soon as arrangements are made for the Brule band, I will be trying to find her and the other captives."

"I will pray for her . . . and thee on your journey to find her."

"We will take any help we can get," he said.

"And thee wishes us to help with settling these poor people on your ranch?"

"Yes, some of it may involve assisting Dr. Weintraub with treating patients, if they'll let him help them."

"I will certainly do what I can. I will speak to the others, but I am confident they will be a part of this. Will thou need help at the village with bringing them back?"

"We're working on that."

"When are thou leaving?"

"Noon tomorrow, if we can."

"I have a horse, and I can ride. Where do we meet?"

"Well, that wouldn't be necessary."

She gave him a look that could kill.

"Meet at Fletcher's Livery."

5

ETHAN, AFTER SOMETHING of a fuss with Running Fox, had finally gotten the boy settled in the spare bedroom. It was a small log-walled house with a single open room that included a small kitchen with a black iron stove-oven at one end and a stone fireplace positioned along the wall near the room's center with a sprawling leather couch in front of it. Two doors at the other end led to the bedrooms. Ethan was glad now to have the extra bedroom, which had not been slept in since the murder of his senior partner, Ben Dobbs, some months back. Dobbs, a lifelong bachelor, had willed his interest in the Lazy R to Ethan. Ben had been like a father to Ethan, who had been raised in a St. Louis orphanage, where he had received a good education before catching a wagon train west at age sixteen.

Ben was a contract scout for the army when Ethan signed on as Chief of Scouts at Fort Laramie following a scouting tour of duty at Fort Kearny. The chief's position was acquired largely because of his ability to read and write and, thus, prepare reports. Ben and the young chief formed a fast friendship over several years of scouting, and each had taken a turn at saving the other's life. Ethan aspired to be a lawyer, however, and eventually, when he read an advertisement in a Cheyenne newspaper for a law clerk placed by a Lockwood lawyer, he approached the elderly attorney, Horace Weatherby, about reading the law in his office. This ultimately led to his being admitted to the territorial bar and, upon Weatherby's retirement, the sole member of his own law firm.

Shortly after passing the bar, the three sections initially making up the Lazy R came up for sale, and Ethan put up a down payment and contacted Ben who joined him as a partner in the ranching operation. Ben's murder by the same men involved in the lynching of the Indian boys was still painful to remember.

Ethan sat at the kitchen table now with his young foreman, and only off-season cowhand, Joe Hollings, blond and baby-faced, who looked even younger than his twenty-five years. Fall and winter, Joe was the sole occupant of the five-bed bunkhouse, although Ethan had offered him a room in the ranch house, since he took his meals there anyway. The cowboy had politely declined.

As they sipped at their steaming coffees, they discussed ranch affairs first. "I think it's time to take on another full-time hand," Ethan said, "maybe somebody who could double as a cook." He and Joe shared cooking chores, and neither would have been hired on to run a chuck wagon.

"I've been thinking the same thing, but I hated to bring it up, since I don't have to pay the bills."

"Most cowhands I know would be insulted to double up as a cook."

"Depends on how hungry they are."

Ethan looked at Joe suspiciously. "You wouldn't have somebody in mind, by chance?"

Joe returned a sheepish grin. "I got a damn good prospect who's been sleeping in the bunkhouse the past few days. He dropped by while you were up to the Sioux village. Wanted to know if we had any work for some meals. Well, Boss, I said he could help out till you got back. He helped me round up strays and put up some hay. The man knows work, let me tell you. And, with all due respect, Boss, he did all the cooking, and we ate high on the hog here the last few days."

"If he's such a gourmet chef, why the hell didn't you have him fix supper tonight?"

"Well, I thought it might be kind of strange to have a new cook in the kitchen without you even knowing about him."

"Tell me about this guy."

"Well, l he's a few years older than me. He was an army cook at some fort in Texas before he switched to cavalry. Fought Comanche for a few years and worked on a ranch down in north Texas after that for a spell, until there was some trouble."

"What kind of trouble?"

Hollings was quiet, like he was struggling for words. "Well, you see, this fella is a colored man. Some of the cowboys didn't like working with a 'nigger' . . . his words, not mine."

"I see. I don't suppose that's helped him find a job in the cow business since?"

"He didn't say as much, but I figure that's why he came north. Probably found the pickings wasn't much better."

"Did you tell him about what's going to be happening here? The Sioux moving in and all?"

"I did."

"What did he say?"

"He just said, 'that ought to be interesting.'"

"I'd like to meet this man. Why don't you run over to the bunkhouse and invite this man in for coffee?"

Hollings returned less than ten minutes later, followed by a lanky, sinewy man with flawless mahogany-colored skin, who wore a wide-brimmed Plainsman hat tilted down on his forehead. The cowhand removed his hat when he entered the room, and Ethan stood and offered his hand, which the man accepted with a firm grip. "I'm Ethan Ramsey," Ethan said. "Joe says you're looking for work."

"My name's Jeb Oaks, and yes, sir, I'm looking for work." The cowhand met Ethan's eyes steadily.

"Let's sit down at the kitchen table and talk about it over coffee . . . although from what Joe tells me, my offering's going to taste like mud."

"No such thing as bad coffee, sir. Folks just have different tastes. Of course, when we were in the field chasing Comanche, we were just glad to grab a cup once in a while." Ethan noted a soft southern drawl in the man's voice.

Joe and Jeb pulled up chairs at the kitchen table, while Ethan retrieved another cup of coffee. Ethan placed a steaming cup in front of Jeb and sat down. "Tell me about your army background."

"Not much to tell. I served as a First Sergeant with Mackenzie's Tenth Cavalry . . . buffalo soldiers they called us . . . but being an Army Scout, you likely know all about that."

"I do. A highly-decorated outfit that served with distinction."

"We spent most of our time chasing Quanah. Never quite caught him, but, mark my word, the Comanche wars are close to being over."

"You've worked cows, and Joe says you cook?"

"Yes, sir. If it helps, I can read and write. My mother is Cherokee, and I was educated in Quaker schools near the village. I'm fair with numbers and know some about bookkeeping. I'm not in a position right now to be too fussy about what I do."

"Well, Jeb, I might be able to make use of all of your skills at the Lazy R. Did Joe tell you about our immediate problem?"

"Moving a tribe of Sioux onto your ranch for the winter . . . sort of a private reservation, so to speak?"

"Yes, and then, after that, I'm heading north along the Powder River to look for some young women who were taken captive during the raid on the Sioux village. Joe's going to have to stay here to coordinate sheltering and feeding of the Sioux with volunteers from town. Would you consider helping with moving of the Indians down the mountain . . . and then riding with me on the search for the women? With the promise of a full-time job when we get back, of course."

"This search you're talking about sounds a mite dangerous."

"It is. And you've still got a job here if you don't want to take that on. We need help here at the ranch, and it wouldn't be fair for me to make my trip north a condition to your getting a job here. Your background just suggests that you might have some skills that would help if I run into a hornet's nest."

"Like being able to kill a man?"

"Yes, but you might have some ideas for strategy when we catch up to these killers."

"If we catch up," the former soldier said doubtfully.

"When."

"Yes, sir. I guess I'll ride along."

"I'm glad to hear that. And you don't need to call me 'sir.' Ethan will do just fine."

"Yes, sir."

6

AFTER JOE AND Jeb returned to the bunkhouse, Ethan dumped a flour sack full of mail and messages on the table. His secretary, Katherine Wyeth, had sorted the messages and mail and placed them neatly on his desk in order of importance, based upon her system, which was still mostly a mystery to him. Katherine, a matronly woman in her mid-sixties, had come with the office when he read the law with old Horace Weatherby and, later, acquired the practice. She was nothing if not efficient, and after a rocky start, they now tolerated each other reasonably well. Some days they might even approach an uneasy friendship. He had not built a stepping stone to the betterment of their relationship, however, when he appeared at the office and unceremoniously swept the organized papers into the sack.

He shuffled through the mail first since there was not a lot of it. There were not any bills since Katherine had authority to write checks on his office bank account and took care of payment of the accounts, unless there were insufficient funds on deposit to cover the checks, in which event he heard from her immediately. Unfortunately, this was more than an occasional occurrence. Horace Weatherby had surrendered his practice because he was dying of consumption. Otherwise, the venerable, silver-maned lawyer had informed Ethan he would have hung on. Small town lawyers did not retire, Weatherby warned—they survived, until death knocked. Sort of like ranching, Ethan thought.

Ethan noticed a thick legal-size envelope with a return address indicating it was from "Johnathan David Jordan, Esquire, Attorney and Counselor" of Cheyenne. Of course, the title was just a fancy way of the man calling himself a lawyer. Ethan supposed it impressed a few, but he always found the self-designation a bit pompous. He brushed some of the clutter aside, opened the envelope, and pulled out the contents.

There was another smaller envelope inside, sealed with wax, no less. There were also some yellowed parchment sheets that appeared to have crude maps of some kind scratched on them. He plucked out a crisp white sheet that turned out to be the lawyer's letterhead and began to read.

Dear Mr. Ramsey: I am the attorney for the estate of the late Pierre dePaul, and I was also appointed executor of his will. Mr. dePaul died several years ago, but his estate has been held open pending his sole beneficiary, Miss Skye dePaul, attaining the age of 21 years. That significant event occurred in June. I last received correspondence from Miss dePaul approximately one month past when she informed me that you are her personal legal counsel and that I should send any future communications regarding her business to your office.

Mr. dePaul owned a small ranch, containing no more than 160 acres on the outskirts of Cheyenne. While the property presently produces mostly scrub trees and wildlife, the location is directly in the path of Cheyenne's growth, and, in the years ahead, it will likely prove to be a sound investment. Mr. dePaul also claimed to own another property in Northern Wyoming on which he operated a trading post at one time. Unfortunately, I have uncovered no evidence of recorded title for any such real estate, and I suspect it was just something he claimed based upon that nebulous term some settlers have called 'squatter's rights.' The maps enclosed with this letter purport to establish the location of the property, although I confess I cannot make sense of them. Miss dePaul would succeed to her father's inter-

est, whatever that might be. She should have no great expectation, however.

I will now close the probate and transfer the Cheyenne property to Miss dePaul's name. I will make appropriate provision in the court decree to cover any property that may be hereafter discovered. The livestock, personal effects and other chattels have been liquidated, and, after payment of my fees and court costs, there should be about $5200 in the estate account. Miss dePaul previously provided me with her banking information, and I will transfer the funds in the estate account to her personal account in the First Bank of Cheyenne.

While her inheritance does not make her a wealthy woman, it should provide her with a nice stake, and, if prudently managed, can be helpful to her in the years ahead.

Finally, I should mention the sealed envelope. Pierre dePaul wanted this to be opened only after his daughter attained the age of majority. Since she designated her own legal counsel, I did not feel comfortable opening the envelope. Thus, I place it in your hands for disposition at your discretion.

Please advise if I can be of assistance, or if you prefer I proceed in some other fashion. In the meantime, I am your Obedient Servant. Most sincerely, Jonathan David Jordan.

Ethan picked up the sealed envelope and examined it thoughtfully. He guessed Skye still thought of him as her lawyer since her contact with Jordan had occurred subsequent to their parting at his office in Lockwood. Of course, at this moment he had no idea whether his client was alive. Should he open the envelope or not? Somehow, to do so seemed an invasion of Skye's privacy. On the other hand, if the contents had legal implications, they might disclose something he should be aware of. And if Skye was dead, as seemed quite likely, what difference did it make?

He opened the penknife he'd set on the table, and, after a moment's hesitation, slipped the blade beneath the envelope's flap and carefully sliced it open. He eased the stiff sheet of paper from the envelope, unfolded it, and then tried to decipher the crude, thick-inked letters spread almost haphazardly across the page and began to read:

Deer Skye. I be dead if yu see this. I hav many egels and duble egels at old treding post. For yu. Get trusty person to help fin. Rememer bager? Luv. Papa.

Ethan got up and tossed a few more logs in the fireplace where the fire had nearly burned itself out, leaving only a few smoldering coals. Then he sat back down at the table and picked up the letter again and studied it before he looked at the maps. A treasure hunt now, too? The "egels" in the note were obvious references to the ten dollar-eagle and twenty dollar-double eagle gold coins minted by the United States government. The mystery was intriguing but low on his list of priorities. He guessed that the maps were essentially intended to show the reader how to find the old trading post, which seemed to be located on what most called the Powder River. Everything came back to the river, and Ethan decided at that moment the search for Skye would start on the Powder River.

7

E THAN SAT ASTRIDE Patch surveying the village
that was coming to life on the brown grass of a
pasture less than a quarter mile from the Lazy
R ranch buildings. The barn had been converted to a
headquarters and warehouse for supplies, and Joe Hollings and Rachael Cooper had teamed up to run the operation. Joe had obviously been instantly enamored with
the young Quaker woman, and, while she seemed equally
attracted to Joe, Ethan hoped she did not end up breaking his heart. Sometimes Joe was a man who seemed too
gentle and good for this rugged country.

Rachael had acquitted herself well on the journey to
and from Lame Buffalo's village. She had not overstated
her skills as a horsewoman, and her empathy and tire-
less caring for the old and ill had been critical to moving the mass of people down the mountain trail. His new

cowhand, Jeb Oaks, had proved his worth as well. Not only did the man have an uncanny way with horses, he showed signs of being a natural leader. He did not wait for orders to attend to an urgent task. If a problem came up, he set about solving it, and where help was needed, he recruited. Ethan found it interesting that the whites on the mission did not resist Jeb's gentle urging to a task. Somehow competence had a way of winning out over prejudice, it seemed. Occasionally, Jeb and Otter had bumped heads, but they soon carved out their own niches in the order of things.

Ethan had been amazed to find more than a dozen Lockwood men at the livery when they rendezvoused for the trek to the village. More than half were volunteer firemen recruited by Sheriff Will Bridges, but others were local cowhands sent by their ranch bosses. There were those who disapproved, of course, and some of these watched with scorn and frowning faces when the rescue party rode out. But Ethan's pessimism about his fellow man was abated for a time.

As makeshift shelters of canvas and salvaged skins began to rise on the grassy floor of the valley, Ethan felt comfortable leaving the Brule refugees in the hands of the team of volunteers. It was time to find Skye or, at least, learn about her fate. He saw Jeb riding away from the buildings on a spotted Appaloosa gelding, with two pack mules in tow, along with a thickly-muscled, sorrel stallion called Razorback. The latter was for Skye. He was a contrary animal, who would bite if given the chance, and was prone to throwing a rider who let his guard down. As a prank, Ethan had once challenged Skye to ride the animal, and, of course, Razorback had been docile as a house kitten in her hands and earned his way to becoming her favorite horse.

His toughest job had been a pint-sized one—Running Fox. The boy still did not want to let Ethan out of sight. He had insisted upon joining the relief party to the Brule village, even though Ethan argued to have him stay at the Lazy R with Joe. Since that mission did not seem likely to be dangerous, Ethan had relented, and he had to admit the boy had been useful in cajoling and reassuring younger members of the Brule band during the course of the journey.

But Ethan conceded he had been less than adept at asserting his adult authority over the boy. Having been raised in an orphanage, perhaps he had not learned how to exercise fatherly discipline. Of course, the boy was not his son. Surely someone in the band would take him in, if he just stayed behind. Regardless, this trip was no place for a boy, and he explained that to Running Fox this morning. He needed to pick up the maps and Pierre de-Paul's letter at the house where the boy was to stay with Rachael during Ethan's absence. He seemed to get along well with the young Quaker woman, and although Skye had taught him the rudiments of English with a limited vocabulary, Rachael was determined to recruit him as a pupil for the Pennock School when things were more settled. She would start the polishing, she said.

As Jeb approached, Ethan nudged Patch toward him. "Razorback give you any trouble?" Ethan asked.

"Nothing but. That animal is one mean son of a bitch. He would have took a chunk out of my shoulder if I hadn't had my buckskin jacket on. You're the boss, but this horse wouldn't have been my pick for company."

"He likes the lady we're looking for . . . and she likes him."

"Well, I guess everybody needs to have somebody."

"They don't come any tougher. He's been practically resurrected from the dead. Some months back he was shot out from under Skye. I found him in the woods at night, stretched out with a bullet wound in his neck. I left him for dead. A week later, he staggered into the ranch yard. Doc Weintraub, our local medical doctor, was pressed into vet duties and removed the bullet. Two weeks later, the ornery devil was back in stud service."

Ethan continued, "I'd like to get out of Lockwood mid-morning. I need to pick up something at the house, and then we'll swing by the sheriff's office before we head into the mountains."

Ethan quickly retrieved his papers at the ranch house while Running Fox watched silently. He wore his breech-clout, although it served no function, since he had acquiesced to wearing a pair of blue denims and a plaid shirt Rachael had picked up at the general store. The moccasins were fine, Ethan thought, but with weather due to turn colder anytime, he did not want the boy running around half naked anymore.

As Ethan eased into the saddle, Running Fox stood on the porch with Rachael, his face sober. Ethan gave him a little wave. "I'll be back soon, Running Fox. You help Rachael while we're gone."

"May God go with thee," Rachael said.

"Good-bye, Puma," the boy added softly.

8

THEY STOOD ON the boardwalk in front of Sheriff Bridges's office. "Ethan, you're a damned fool going after that small army with just the two of you."

"They'll hear us . . . or see us if we have too many riders. A posse would never get close enough . . . or they'd get too close and get ambushed."

"But what the hell do you do if you catch them?"

"We'll figure that out when we get there."

"I've got a thought, Ethan. I know somebody who would be a hell of a handy man for something this crazy."

Ethan eyed the Sheriff suspiciously. "And who might that be?"

"One Ball McLarty."

"One Ball? What kind of a name is that?"

"That's all anybody knows him by. He's an old mountain man, who came out here in the late twenties or early thirties, when all we had was beavers and other such critters. He got the name because three Arapahoe cornered him and got him down and sliced out his left nut, before he got pissed and killed the three of them. For years, he wore a necklace with six dried up balls strung on it around his neck. 'A ball for a ball,' he says. He's proud of his name and says the squaws love his one ball, and it works just fine."

Jeb said, "Sounds like one tough hombre to me."

"That's probably an understatement. Only thing is, I can't vouch for his honesty. Don't know him too good, but he may be a little short of scruples."

"Will, if he's been out here since the twenties, this guy's older than hell," Ethan said.

"I don't know. I suppose he could be in his seventies. I saw him a few months back, though, and I think he could still whip a grizzly bear in a fair fight. He can use a rifle better than any man alive . . . says he uses a Sharps these days. But the important thing to you is he knows northern Wyoming and southern Montana like the back of his hand. As I recollect, Ethan, your scouting days was spent in southern Wyoming and Colorado and Nebraska."

"Why do you think he'd help us?"

"Money. He ain't interested in charity work."

"Forget it. I can hardly meet expenses these days."

"Wait a minute." Bridges stepped away and went into his office, returning shortly with something in his hand. He extended the hand to Ethan and opened it.

"A double eagle. What's this for?"

"One Ball McLarty. He'll do anything for this kind of money."

"I can't take your money for this, Will."

"It's from my county contingency fund. I can spend it however I like. I think this is a good investment. You can pay it back someday if it bothers you."

"You really think the old guy's worth this?"

"He'll earn it in a fight. Just keep him on your side."

"Where do we find this great man?"

"You know where the Jack Rabbit Trail is?"

"Yes. You pick it up in the foothills, and it winds up into the mountains northwest. Steep, and a bit narrow at places for comfort."

"You'll find his cabin about two hours up the trail. It's not visible from the trail, but an old Army Scout like yourself will find the turnoff to your right."

"He doesn't sound like a social animal."

"Let's say he likes to pick his own company."

Ethan plucked the gold coin from the sheriff's palm. "We'll stop and have a chat with this gentleman. His place is pretty much on our way."

9

THE TURNOFF TO One Ball McLarty's cabin was over a rocky ridge that revealed no prints, horse or human, but as Ethan surveyed the surrounding forest, his eyes picked up a break in the trees that might be a serviceable passageway. They dismounted and let the horses blow and rest while they drank from their canteens.

"That was a hell of a climb, Boss," Jeb said. "I feel sort of guilty drinking in front of these horses. Always bothered me when I was out on the plains in Comanche country, too."

Ethan pointed to the break in the trees. "There will be water for the horses at the end of the path over there. A man wouldn't put up a cabin far from water." Ethan continued to study the landscape for a few minutes. "My guess is that this old codger already knows we're here.

We'll just lead the horses through the trees, and sooner or later, he'll make himself known."

They headed toward the break, and, as suspected, they found a narrow path that allowed them to pass through the woods single-file, pushing back the scratchy pine branches from their necks and faces as they moved. Razorback resisted and planted his feet several times, so Ethan let loose of Patch's reins, knowing his horse would plod forward, and moved to the end of the pack string. He tied a strip of rawhide to Razorback's halter, and then, like a caboose at the end of a train, led the temperamental beast, without further rebellion, following the others.

The pungent scent of wood smoke drifted into the undergrowth, and Ethan hoped it was a sign of a fireplace doing its work. The smell grew stronger as they walked, so he figured they were moving in the right direction. After what he guessed to be a half mile of weaving through the forested tunnel, he saw daylight ahead and Patch breaking into a clearing with Jeb and his horse directly behind. Ethan soon joined them at the site of a rather large log cabin with a nearby low-roofed barn. The structures appeared to be the result of master craftsmanship. The clearing was surprisingly expansive, with probably four or five acres of meadow surrounding the building site, Ethan guessed—a good strategy for defending the occupant against unwelcome visitors. A clear mountain stream snaked its way through the meadow, rushing over a narrow, rocky bed, affording the occupants a reliable water supply.

"Stretch those hands way high and step ten paces away from your critters. Don't want to kill no innocent animal." The menacing voice came from behind them, near the path they had just exited. The man spoke softly but with a tone that left no doubt he should be taken seriously.

Both Ethan and Jeb obeyed, although Patch was already leading the other horses and mules away for a drink at the stream. Ethan turned but could not see the man. "We're not looking for trouble, mister. We came to see One Ball McLarty about an offer for a job. Sheriff Will Bridges sent us."

"Bridges, huh? What's his wife's name?"

"Martha."

"What's his son's name?"

"He has no children."

A tall, lean man emerged like a specter from the blackness of the forest. He must be only an inch or two under six and a half feet, Ethan estimated, taller with the beaver skin cap that fit like a bowl on his scalp, with flaps that fell over his ears. He wore a fur vest—wolf, perhaps—but his sinewy arms were bare. His face was craggy and covered with several weeks' growth of white whiskers, but the ladies would likely have considered him a handsome man in his younger years. His cobalt-blue eyes were alert and fierce as he approached with his Sharps lifted and ready to fire. The long-handled, Cheyenne war axe that hung from his belt was not for decoration, Ethan surmised.

"What's your handle?"

"Ethan Ramsey."

"Heard of you. Goddamned law wrangler. Be a waste of a good bullet." He turned to Jeb. "Who's the darky? Your slave?"

Ethan started to give an intemperate reply, but he was cut off by Jeb. "My name is Jebediah Oaks. My friends call me 'Jeb.' You may call me, Mr. Oaks."

McLarty suddenly roared with laughter and lowered his rifle. When he finally caught his breath, he said, "Mr. Oaks it is, then. I think you'll do, Mr. Oaks. You may call me One Ball. And you gentlemen may put your hands down, so long as you don't play with your guns. You got a business proposition, huh? Why don't you fetch your horses and stake them out someplace and come on up to the house, and my woman will get out some biscuits and tea."

When Ethan and Jeb got to the house, One Ball booted the door open and pointed to some split-log chairs that were placed around a rough-topped pine table. The cabin-house consisted of a single massive room, with the table at one end and a huge bed at the other. A large stone fireplace was centered along a wall in between. Other than several bearskin rugs stretched out on the cedar-planked floor and a few buffalo robes tossed on the bed, the cabin was otherwise spartanly furnished, yet very inviting. An Indian woman, who appeared not yet twenty, knelt by a dying fire, lifting the lid of a Dutch oven with an iron rod. Then, evidently satisfied with the results, she hoisted the oven out of the coals and onto the hearth. When she stood, Ethan saw she was quite pretty, although a little on the plump side, and very pregnant.

The young woman set steaming cups of tea at their places. A sip convinced Ethan that he was drinking something pleasurable, likely a concoction made up of native plants. While Ethan told One Ball the story that had led them to his cabin, Yellow Bird, as One Ball called her, smiled pleasantly as she dropped several biscuits on each small plate and gave them a small hunting knife to share for spreading a nondescript jam from a bowl she provided. He wasn't certain how much English the young woman understood, but Ethan spoke to her. "Ma'am, I've never had better biscuits . . . or tea, for that matter."

He meant it, and she responded with a pleased smile and gave a little nod of her head.

"So," One Ball said, "Old Will thinks I should ride along to look after you two. Appears that could take some doin' I fear. How much would I get for this?"

Ethan pulled the double eagle from his pocket and flipped it onto the table. He watched One Ball eye the coin greedily.

"Add an eagle, and I'll do it," One Ball said.

"No, that's it. Take it or leave it."

"In advance. I'll give it to Yellow Bird in case I don't come back."

Ethan found it hard to argue with that, but he still didn't quite trust the old weasel. But they really needed another man. "It's yours. We want to strike out on the trail as soon as possible . . . no later than morning."

"I want another night with my woman, and your critters could use some rest. You camp out under those pines in front of the cabin. We'll ride out at first light. I'll take my woman to her village . . . she's Cheyenne, you know. Her band's a day's ride north of here. She wanted to be with her mama and her people when she birthed the child, anyways. You keep going on the Jack Rabbit Trail till you reach the Powder. I'll find you there in about two days. You've already climbed the steepest of it. You'll have supper with us. Venison stew, and more biscuits. Ain't no woman can cook like my squaw . . . and she can do a lot more." The old mountain man winked. "Cost me five horses, but I got to give her old man two more if she births a boy. Makes no difference to me, but a girl child would be cheaper."

Supper had turned out as good as promised, and Ethan and Jeb decided to grab their sleep early, agreeing it might be hard to come by in the days ahead. They laid out their bedrolls, and Ethan dropped quickly into an exhausted sleep. Minutes later, he was startled awake by a grunting that sounded like a grizzly bear tracking a meal. Ethan reached for the Winchester that rested by his buffalo robe blanket.

"You hear that, too?" Jeb whispered.

"Yeah. What is it?"

"Coming from the house."

"The house? Trouble?"

A woman screamed. Then she laughed hysterically. The grunting stopped and was replaced by a low moan that was just short of a growl.

"You don't think?" Ethan whispered.

"I do think. And I may just vomit."

Near morning, Ethan was awakened again by the commotion from the cabin. He pulled the robe over his ears and fell back to sleep.

10

THEY WERE NO more than a few miles from the Powder River when Ethan silently signaled a halt. "I'm going to dismount," he said softly. "You take Patch and move on up the trail a half mile or so. I'll circle back on foot and see who's following us."

"I didn't hear anything," Jeb said.

"I didn't, either. I feel it." Ethan peeled off his boots and removed a pair of well-worn, calf-high moccasins from his saddlebags, replacing them with the boots. He slipped on the moccasins and, after pulling his rifle from its scabbard, waved Jeb forward. "Have a gun ready just in case I run into something I can't handle."

Jeb headed his caravan up the trail as Ethan disappeared into the forest. Ethan weaved easily and soundlessly through the trees, working his way back a little less than a hundred yards, and then he sat down some twenty feet off the trail, resting his back against a sturdy pine tree, waiting and watching.

A half hour later, he caught sight of a rider slowly moving up the path he and Jeb had taken. Ethan eased to his feet, readying his rifle. Whoever it was seemed to be picking his way cautiously, and Ethan noted the rider maneuvered with some skill and deliberation. At first, he thought it might be One Ball McLarty, but the old mountain man would have no reason to hang back. Besides, McLarty was a formidable physical presence, and this rider sat low in the saddle.

Finally, when the rider swung around a curve in the trail, Ethan recognized him. He leaned his Winchester against the tree, plucked his Bowie knife from its sheath, and inched closer to the trail. When he neared the tree line, he stopped again until the rider passed by, and then he emerged from the curtain of trees, eased behind the unsuspecting rider, grasped his wrist, and swung him roughly off the horse. In a single motion, Ethan had the rider flattened on the rocky ground, straddling his chest with the razor-sharp blade inches from his prey's throat.

Running Fox's eyes widened in terror as they looked up at Ethan and the threatening knife blade. "No, no, no," he said, sobbing, and shaking his head from side to side. "Me Puma's friend. Come to help."

Ethan figured he had scared the boy enough for the moment, and he got up and sheathed the knife, saying nothing but sending a message with the anger in his eyes to the boy that he was not a welcome visitor. This was not a good development. He had to think about this.

He lifted the frightened boy back into the saddle and commenced leading the horse up the trail. At least, he thought, the boy had the good sense not to say anything for now. It was all Ethan could do to restrain himself from giving the kid a good butt whipping.

When they met up with Jeb, Ethan's mood had not improved much, and Jeb seemed to sense it. His eyes fixed on Running Fox, but he said nothing.

Ethan turned to the boy, "Get off the horse. We have to talk."

Running Fox dismounted.

"Sit down," Ethan ordered, pointing to a fallen log that edged the trail.

The boy obeyed, staring at Ethan with his dark, wide eyes, his lips trembling.

Ethan felt his heart softening. Maybe he had overreacted, but he had wanted to teach the boy a lesson. He let himself down on the log a few feet from the boy. "I would never have harmed you. You know that, don't you?"

"Yes. But you make me scared."

"I wanted you to understand what a dangerous thing you did following us. Anybody could have jumped you like that. Now, what are you doing here?"

"Me help Puma find Sky-in-the-Morning."

"No, you are a boy. This is work for grown men. Now we may lose valuable time taking you back. Or if you come with us, we will be distracted trying to protect you. It could cost a man his life. Can you see that?"

"Me not know this word, 'distract.'"

"It means we will be looking after you when we should be watching for something else . . . like someone who wants to kill us."

Ethan abruptly looked up at Jeb, who had his arms folded across his gelding's saddled back, his chin resting on this arms. "Do you want to take him back?"

"We're too short of guns now, Boss. I don't see how you can spare me."

"I know. I'm just trying to avoid the reality of the situation. I guess he goes with us."

Ethan turned back to Running Fox. "Do you understand you did the wrong thing, following us here? Rachael and Otter and the others are going to be worried about you. And you may cause danger for the rest of us, as well as yourself?"

"Me see that. Sorry. Wanted to be with Puma. Scared Puma not come back."

The boy appeared genuinely contrite—and frightened. "Well, the Powder should be only a few miles up the trail. Let's head on up there and find a place to make an early camp. We'll get some rest and wait for One Ball."

11

THEY DID NOT have to wait for One Ball. When the trail feathered out onto the steep, rocky banks of the Powder River, Ethan smelled the sweet smoke of venison roasting over a cooking fire. His nose led him fifty paces up the river bank, where he found the old mountain man, sitting in front of the fire holding a forked stick draped with meat over the hot coals beneath the low flickering flames.

"Venison from a fresh-kilt doe hanging in the trees back there. Ain't along to do the cooking, but you're welcome to the meat." As they dismounted, One Ball's eyes fixed on Running Fox and then turned to Ethan. "Where'd you find the papoose?"

"He's from the village I told you about. He followed us."

"Send him back. I didn't sign on to nursemaid no papoose."

"He's not your responsibility. I'll look after him. He stays."

"Bad luck. He talk American?"

"His English is passable. His name's Running Fox."

"Some kind of a rescue troop we got here . . . a law wrangler, a darky, and a papoose. I didn't bargain for this. I'm thinking maybe I ought to pull up stakes and head home."

"You've been paid in advance. Will Bridges said you were an honorable man . . . that you could be trusted. He also said you were not a coward." Of course, Bridges had not given that strong of an endorsement.

McLarty seemed taken aback by that. "Don't believe everything that old fart tells you." He pulled his venison steak from the coals. The meat was charred but dripping blood. He sniffed it, blew on it and bit off a chunk, chewing vigorously as red rivulets rolled down his chin.

Ethan took this as dismissal, and he nodded to the others to unsaddle and get settled. Soon they had their horses staked out, and after cutting their own cooking implements, joined McLarty at the fire. Ethan noted that Running Fox stayed as far away from McLarty as possible. The boy was evidently afraid of the man and was likely wishing he had stayed at the Lazy R.

"We'll have company by morning," McLarty said.

"What do you mean?" Ethan replied.

"Well, Mr. Puma, you're some kind of a cat. You can't smell them?"

"Smell what?"

"Sioux. The papoose's kind. Headed our way. Allowing for rest, about a half day behind us, I'd say. I'd guess a half dozen, more or less."

"How do you know this?"

McLarty wiped his mouth with his tattered, buckskin shirt sleeve. "I know. And you don't want to bet against it."

"We'll need to post lookouts," Jeb said. "I can take first watch."

"Don't need no lookouts," McLarty said. "I'll know when they're within an hour's ride."

"I don't doubt it," Ethan replied, "but it won't hurt to keep watch."

"Suit yourself. Just don't be waking me up."

12

SKYE DEPAUL SAT in the darkness, her back resting against a towering pine. She shivered occasionally when she became aware of the night's damp chill. The three girls from the village seemed to be sleeping now and were wrapped in the two buffalo robes that had been tossed into their shrub and tree-shrouded natural enclave. Skye would share one of the robes later, but now she had to think.

She had to sweep her mind of the hate that crowded out clarity, but it was a challenge. Repeatedly, throughout the past several days of their encampment here, the barbarians, as she thought of them, had dragged the sixteen-year-olds, Prairie Flower and Antelope, and eighteen-year-old She-Bear, from the little clearing and passed them among the men, like so much food or drink, for satisfying their carnal pleasures. Only Skye had been left untouched, and it perplexed and troubled her. She felt guilty, in a way, that she was not sharing the depredations of her companions, and even though she was an old one-armed woman of twenty-one, she had seen no pickiness in the tastes of these lowly animals when they pillaged the village.

A coyote howled in the distance, followed by excited yipping of others of his pack. It made her think of her uncle, Lame Buffalo, and his vision on what he called "the night of the coyote." She wondered if he had survived the attack on the village. She had watched with sickening horror as an axe split the skull of her mother, Singing Lark, but she had not seen her uncle during the melee. The coyote, of course, turned her mind also to Ethan Ramsey. She knew he was going to ask her to marry him when she had cut him short at their last meeting. And she had wanted to see him again when she left him an unsigned bank draft for his legal fees, hoping he would see she was sending him an excuse to seek her out.

The realization of her love for Ethan had struck her at an inopportune time. She had just lost her left arm below the elbow. How could she be certain that Ethan's feelings were not just misplaced sympathy? How was she going to adapt to this change in her life? Love notwithstanding, she was not going to be any man's helpless wife. She loved him. Maybe he loved her. If she became convinced he truly did, she would then consider whether they could make a life together. It was all a moot question now anyway. The chances of her surviving to see Ethan again were remote—unless they could escape.

Escape. She had thought of little else since her abduction with the others from the village. There were so many of the barbarians. Men were in and out of the camp, so it was difficult to get a count, but she thought there were at least seventeen. There seemed to always be several sentries on duty, and there was a loose military structure to the camp's activity. Clearly, the leader was the one they called "Captain." Captain Quint was a swarthy man with shoulder-length black hair and a pencil-thin moustache. She guessed he might be thirty-five years old, and his trim, muscular body and bearing suggested a man who took care of himself and might be a bit vain about his appearance. He was of average height but always stood out among this otherwise rag-tag bunch of men. She felt his eyes upon her constantly and sensed that some type of confrontation between them was coming soon.

She would not leave without the others. They had already endured too much. They had been delivered a death sentence whether they knew it or not. She-Bear would leap at the opportunity. Tall and lithe, she was a feisty one, as attested by her name. She had not resisted the abuse by the barbarians only because of Skye's counsel to do what was necessary to survive, so that she might live free again. She had attended the Quaker school and spoke English well, which she did not even hint to her captors so that her ears might hear something that might help their escape. The other two girls were shy and frightened and spoke only a smattering of the white man's tongue. Skye feared they were too accepting of their fate and held out hope they would eventually become wives to someone among the ruthless men. Skye knew it was a foolish hope. And who would want to be the wife of any man who was a part of this sorry tribe?

Skye started at a stirring in the grass nearby. She turned and saw it was She-Bear, who quickly moved in beside her. "I heard the Captain talking to one of the buffalo hairs who waited for his turn to mount me. He is going to take you from our nest tomorrow. He is going to talk with you. It sounds important. They are looking for something and think you know where to find it."

"I cannot imagine what that would be. I can think of nothing I know that these men would be interested in."

"Tomorrow is the last day at this place, I think. They will be moving north. We should make our escape."

"Our only hope is the river. We veered east of it when we moved to this camp. I think it should be no more than a mile from here. I would like to cross it to the west side and then follow it south. It will eventually lead to a village of some tribe or of the whites. Either would be better than where we are now."

"They will follow us."

"If we must, we can enter the water and let it carry us away."

"That would be dangerous. It runs fast, and it is cold. We could die."

"Nothing could be more dangerous than remaining with these men."

"Yes, that is true."

"Tomorrow night. There are no signs that these barbarians are planning to move out in the morning. And if this Captain Quint wishes to speak with me, perhaps I should hear his words. I may learn something of value."

"He probably plans to mount you and pierce you with his spear."

"I am prepared for whatever happens."

"We should not tell Prairie Flower or Antelope of our plans until we are ready to leave. I fear they may tell the evil men to try to court their favor. They can no longer be trusted."

Skye thought about this. "You are right. And I cannot fault them. They want to live at any price. I fear that if they choose to remain with these men, their path will still lead to death, or worse. We must give them an opportunity to go with us, but if they will not, we will go without them." She hesitated, "Can you fire a rifle?"

"I have used one. My brother allowed me to use a rifle he took from a white man once. I fired the weapon with greater accuracy than my brother, and it angered him. I believe I can load the weapon and shoot it and kill these animals with it."

"We should try to obtain a rifle. I have fired a rifle many times but not since I lost my hand. I think it would be difficult for me without much practice. A pistol, I could make use of, I think."

"I will obtain weapons before we escape."

"How would you do this?"

"I will take them from one of the sentries. I have a knife I slipped from a sheath on a white raider's belt while he was spearing me. Men are such fools. When a woman's nest takes over their heads, they think only with their spears. You will see. I will lift my skirt for a sentry, and he will receive a knife in his belly in return. I will then help myself to his weapons."

Skye gave a wry smile. "There is much truth in what you say. I may be able to use a similar strategy."

13

THE MIDDAY SUN was warming Skye's back when Antelope returned to the enclave from servicing some of the raiders. She was a very pretty girl and evidently gave special pleasures to her captors, perhaps even showing some feigned enthusiasm, Skye surmised, for she was clearly most in demand. She doubted Prairie Flower, a fearful, timid soul, would have been more than submissive to the rapists, and she knew that She-Bear, though a remarkably beautiful young woman, was simply passive, deliberately sending a message to her assaulter that he was tolerated only because of his power over her life. Her aura would be one of contempt, and, though the bruises on her face and body indicated she had been beaten more brutally than her friends, her spirit was undamaged.

Moments after Antelope sat down next to Prairie Flower on one of the robes, a towering black man stepped into the clearing. His eyes immediately fastened on Skye. "Captain wants you . . . now."

Skye tossed a glance at She-Bear, who nodded her encouragement. "I will follow you," Skye told the man, summoning up her courage to show a brave front despite the fear that danced down her spine.

The black man led her away from the clearing and through the camp, where the raiders loitered, some playing cards, others napping. She caught their knowing leers as she walked, her head held high and her body erect. She could feel them eyeing her naked thigh and bare shoulder, where her doeskin dress had been ripped apart. She wished she could spit on them, but she focused on keeping her face stoic and expressionless. At the far end of the campsite they came to a canvas military tent, one of a half dozen set up for those fortunate enough to latch on to the shelter. She supposed there was some informal hierarchy within the barbarian ranks that dictated entitlement to the more luxurious accommodations.

Captain Quint sat on an upright sawed log in front of the open tent. He stared at her with dark, foreboding eyes, his mouth set grim. He spoke to the black man. "Dismissed, Goliath. I'll call when I'm done with the bitch."

Skye wondered if the man's name was a nickname or a mother's prediction of what he was to become. Perhaps, he had been a large baby. Regardless, she would be hugely disappointed if she knew the kind of man he had become.

Captain Quint pointed at a shorter upright log. "Sit down, bitch. I've got questions."

She obeyed, noting that her position, not more than a half dozen feet from the man, left her looking up at him, clearly subservient. Subject to king. Except, she suddenly noticed, he held a riding quirt in his hand instead of a jeweled scepter. "I cannot imagine what questions you might have of me, but I will listen and answer if I am able."

"Goddamned right you will. Or I'll beat you to death. First, what's your name?"

"I am called Sky-in-the-Morning by my people."

"Don't play dumb with me, bitch. I don't give a shit what those filthy animals call you. You have another name."

"In the white man's world, I am known as Skye de-Paul,"

"That's more like it. And your old man's name?"

"My father's name was Pierre dePaul. He died several years ago."

"I know he's dead. If I'd found him while he was alive you wouldn't be here. I would've got my answers from him. Of course, he'd still be dead."

"I am sorry. I do not understand what this is about."

"Your father was a goddamn thief. That's what it's about."

"You still make no sense to me. You are suggesting that he stole something. I find that hard to believe. I knew him as an honest and forthright man."

"You didn't really know him then. He was a thief."

"What did he steal?" She could see him building into a rage at her response.

Captain Quint stood up. "You're playing dumb with me, bitch. I warned you not to do that." His arm swung down, and the tentacles of the quirt struck her face full force, tipping her backward, and the log toppled over and tossed her on the ground. She clumsily got on her knees and balanced herself on her hand as she struggled to get up, but before she could get leverage, the quirt came down harshly on her bare shoulder and flattened her on the earth. Then a booted foot dug into her ribs, sending a shockwave through her body. She made no further effort to move, trying to recoup her strength and deciding to wait for a cue from her attacker.

The man's rage seemed to abate after the outburst. He had been breathing heavily, and his face had turned scarlet, but she sensed his breathing slowing, and a calming force seemed to be taking over. He righted her log stool and took his throne again, she noted, and as she lay there on the ground, she observed he seemed to be pondering something.

"Get up," he said, his voice softer now. "Sit down. Now that you see I am a serious man, maybe you'll tell me the truth."

She touched her face, and her hand came back blood-coated. Her cheeks and shoulder stung like hot coals were pressed against her flesh where the quirt had left its marks. She crawled to her crude seat, and, with no small effort, finally took her place.

"Now, I want you to tell me about the gold," he said, his face masked with a gentler, pleading look.

"Captain, I have no reason not to help you. I am totally at your mercy." She took a deep breath. "I know I must please you if I am to have any hope of living. I will try to answer your questions, but you may have to guide me. I will also pleasure you later, if you desire. I know Sioux secrets of lovemaking that make a man never content with a white woman again." She saw the rise in his britches and the lust in his eyes and quickly returned to the questions that were troubling him. "But, first, I must satisfy your curiosity about the matters you want to know about. Please, tell me what it is you seek from me. I will try to answer."

"You know that ugly stump of an arm you got puts a man off at first, but, otherwise, you're a delicious-looking woman. When I look at you now, it don't take long to get past that. None of the other boys have had you yet. I like the notion of being the first. You play your cards right, and maybe I'll let you be just my woman for a spell."

Skye gave a small, seductive smile and fluttered her eyelashes just a bit. "You're the only man here I would let touch me without a fight. I think we can come to terms . . . now your questions."

"I want to know about the gold."

"Gold?"

"The gold your father stole."

"I will help you if I can. Perhaps there is something in my memory that I can connect to this gold. I seem to be an important link to this gold. It does you no good to kill me, if you need me to help find it. And I cannot enjoy any gold if I am dead. Can you tell me about it?"

He seemed to be studying her, probing for the truth. "This gold was in a strong box. Fifty thousand dollars of gold eagles and double eagles. A fortune. Me and a friend by the name of Scully Patton was a part of Quantrill's raiders back in Missouri, but we broke off with some of the bunch and rode west to Colorado to fight the Yankees there. We mostly took out supply trains, payroll wagons and the like. Then we got wind of a strongbox of gold coins being shipped east out of Laramie. How in the hell the gold come to be at Fort Laramie I could never figure. Made no sense."

She was reluctant to interrupt, but she had to keep him on course and appear interested if she was going to discover what she expected him to know. "But I don't see what any of this has to do with my father. He wasn't even involved in the war."

"Hold your damned horses. I'll come to that. Anyway, the army hid the strongbox with a supply wagon headed to Fort Riley, Kansas. Stupid shitheads. Why would a supply wagon be moving east from Laramie? Every goddamned fool knows that supplies moved from east to west in those times . . . mostly true today. They had a ten-trooper escort. We had twice that many armed men who'd seen the bloodiest fighting of the war. Three days out of Laramie, we overrode those bastards like a swarm of bees. Left all the troopers for buzzard food, and we didn't lose a man. Our problems came a week later when we was camped along the Platte. Things turned nasty when everybody got to arguing about dividing up the gold. The war had pretty much petered out by this time, so it wouldn't do no good to give the money to the Confederacy. Me and Scully planned the raid and decided we was entitled to most of it. The rest of the bunch could hardly wipe their asses without being told to."

Skye said, "Some men lead; others follow. It's that simple. You're a leader. I can see that here in the camp. Nobody would question who's in charge."

Captain Quint looked pleased and nodded his head in agreement. "Well, that's the way it was when we got the gold, but some of the greedy bastards took a notion there ought to be an even split. We was about to come to some blood-letting, when one of our scouts came riding in like the devil was after him. He said that a full company of cavalry was no more than a mile away. Scully and I had already agreed that he and a half dozen trusted men would take off with the gold, head north by way of east Wyoming and meet up with me in Deadwood. I was to tell the rest of the boys we'd meet in Denver to make the split. If I stayed with them, they'd figure we wasn't going to pull no shenanigans. So, I took off with the main

bunch and let the soldiers chase us, and Scully peeled off
and headed north with the gold. I never saw him again."

"So, he kept the gold?"

"That's what I thought at first. Hard for me to believe.
We'd been friends since we was boys in southeast Missouri. We was like brothers. I did everything just like we
planned. Troopers killed some of our fighters, and I finally made it to Denver with eight men. I put on a show
of waiting for Scully and then, after a few weeks, slipped
away and made my way up to Deadwood. Scully never
showed up. After six months I gave up, and, until a year
ago, I made my way hiring out my guns on both sides
of the law. Most of this outfit I recruited to back up a
rancher in a range war."

"What happened a year ago?"

"I was in a saloon in Cheyenne when in walks one of
the guys who was supposed to go to Deadwood with Scully. I cornered him damned fast, believe me, and we had
ourselves a serious talk. Chester's story was that Scully's
bunch was attacked by Cheyenne in northern Wyoming,
and he was the only one that escaped with his scalp. He
didn't know what happened to the gold. Knowing Chester, the cowardly bastard probably took off like a bullet at
the first sign of Indians and left the others to take up the

fight. After our talk, he went and had a mishap and shot hisself in the back of the head later that night."

"But you still didn't know what happened to the gold?"

"No, but I was cozy with some Cheyennes, and I got ahold of an old renegade who hung around town looking for ways to earn a bottle of whiskey. I promised him a case of the poison if he could find out something about what happened to Scully and the gold. It wasn't more than a week and he had the story. It seems a war party did come across Scully and the boys. The Indians were mostly young bucks anxious to collect scalps. They outnumbered Scully's crew and didn't take long to do their slaughtering. Two of the Cheyennes was killed, but they collected scalps from five whites. One got away, and that would have been Chester."

"And the gold? This must be where my father comes in."

"They found a heavy metal box full of coins. They knew it was something white men used to buy things, but they had no use for it. They agreed to take it to a trading post to see if they could trade it for whiskey."

"And they took it to my father's trading post."

"Smart bitch. Now you're catching on to this. They took it to dePaul's. It seems your old man had some kind of understanding with the tribes that he could operate a post out in the middle of this godforsaken country. He'd trade for furs and hides the Indians would bring in and pay in trade goods . . . and a lot of whiskey. Only this time, instead of furs, the old thief traded his whiskey for the gold." Quint's mouth twisted with contempt. "Your old man was no better than any other outlaw. He just didn't use a gun."

"I still don't see what this has to do with me."

"I think you know what happened to the gold."

"But I don't."

"I spent the better part of a year checking out your old man. I know things about him you never would've guessed. He never spent those gold coins. He couldn't while the robbery was fresh in everybody's minds. Even after some years passed he'd still have to be careful . . . dribble the money out a little at a time. Couldn't just walk into a bank and drop a big box of gold coins for deposit."

"I know nothing about this gold. I swear." She saw Quint's face start to cloud up again, and she abruptly stopped her protest. She was only useful to him if he thought she knew something.

Quint continued. "Your old man had a falling out with the Indians about five years later. It seems some of the Sioux and Cheyenne elders started to see his whiskey dealing as trouble. They threatened to burn out his place and told him to get the hell out. He didn't waste no time and left most of his inventory behind. No sign of the gold has showed up yet, and I've had my men check over every inch of the property your thieving old man owned near Cheyenne. Nothing. I think it's at the old trading post."

She had no way of knowing if his conclusions were accurate—whether her father ever had this gold. She remembered the trading post. She had been there once when she was about eleven and again, perhaps, two years later. A few years after that, she remembered her father saying he had closed it up. "You are probably correct," she said.

Quint smiled. It was a charming smile, she thought. The way he changed moods and demeanor was scary. "Now you're making me think that you might not be the stupid bitch I thought you was."

"I remember the trading post. I was there twice. I remember now that my father mentioned some gold he hid there," she lied. "I didn't think it was very much, and I didn't give it any thought. I can't recall where he said he put it. I have to think about it."

"Think hard, bitch. I want an answer tonight."

"Will you share the gold with me? I should get a commission. I think twenty per cent would be fair."

He looked at her incredulously. "You're asking for a commission? How is it you think you can claim a share? You're my prisoner. I can kill you as quick as swatting a fly."

"But if you kill me you won't find the gold."

"You said you didn't know anything about the gold."

"I lied."

He stared at her with a puzzled look on his face, and she met his eyes evenly. "Then you do know."

"I do."

"Then tell me now."

"I will tell you tonight after I pleasure you. I want to convince you we should be partners . . . in business and in pleasure. Come to where I sleep. I will have the robes spread. The others will be gone. You will have a night you will never forget. I promise." She could see the excitement in his eyes—and in his tight britches.

14

A S DUSK'S SHADOWS darkened the slopes of the surrounding mountains, Skye and She-Bear sat on the ground in the women's enclave and spoke softly. A small fire crackled a few feet away, helping to ward off the high-country chill that was quickly descending on the camp. A buffalo robe was spread nearby. Another was bound in a bundle by strips of rawhide She-Bear had pilfered from the camp. Two loose strips were anchored to the others to serve as shoulder straps.

"Your wounds," She-Bear said. "Has my poultice helped? The side of your face looks like it was raked with a grizzly bear's claws. The shoulder is not quite so bad."

"You have endured worse here. So have Antelope and Prairie Flower. I will be fine."

"I have a small bag of things we will need," She-Bear said. "Some jerky . . . for a day or two. A canteen. A nice piece of flint. Other things I thought might be useful. As you asked, I sharpened two sturdy pine sticks about four feet in length. They are next to the fire."

"I see that. What about Antelope and Prairie Flower?"

"They refuse to go with us, but I convinced them it would be dangerous for them to tell. I said the men would probably kill us all if they learned of the plan. They are sharing meals with the raiders now. Antelope was planning to seduce one of the men she likes. If they are with the men, they do not think they can be accused of being a part of the escape."

Skye shook her head doubtfully. "Such things are unpredictable. I still wish they were going with us. These are evil men."

"Are you certain you can get away from this Captain without my help?"

"No. But I hope to kill him. If I can cut off the serpent's head, our escape will be easier. The others may lose interest in tracking us. I doubt if most are even aware of a search for the gold. And if Captain Quint is not alive to pay them, they may give only a token chase. If I do not meet you at the gnarled aspen within a few minutes after you hear a commotion in the camp, do not wait . . . run."

"It is getting dark. I must go capture our weapons."

"Be careful."

"I know the sentry I have selected. He is a little man with a long, hungry spear. He will be grasping to contain his bowels while I cut his throat."

Sometimes she wished She-Bear was less descriptive with her words. She began to pace, nervous with tension, knowing that failure tonight would bring certain death, preceded by unimaginable torture. It seemed like an hour, but she knew it was much less, when she heard the rustling of the brush and tree branches as someone moved along the short path to the enclave.

Captain Quint emerged from the darkness and looked around warily before fastening his eyes on Skye, who had slipped out of her moccasins and was now working her doeskin dress over her head. Momentarily, it fell at her feet, and she stood naked before him. She smiled brazenly. "I am ready to serve your every need, Captain, and then we will talk about gold and our little partnership." She gestured toward the buffalo robe spread on the ground. "Join me here. I will build up the fire."

She tossed a few logs on the fire and poked the points of the long stakes into the coals at the fire's edge. She could see that Quint could not take his eyes off her and was surprised to find that this pleased her somehow.

"I'll be damned, stumpy arm or not, you are one beautiful woman. Maybe we can be partners."

He had already started sliding down his trousers and bent over now to pull off a boot while trying to stand on the other foot. His balance was tenuous, and Skye seized the moment. She plucked up one of the stakes, the pointed end of which had burst into flames, and lunged toward Quint, her strong right arm thrusting forward and driving the stake into his eye. He groaned and stepped backwards as his pants slid down around his knees, tripping him up and slinging him to the rocky ground, leaving him helpless as a turtle on its back. As Quint reflexively pulled the stake from his eye socket, Skye grabbed the other stake and tried to plunge it in his gut. He was rolling in agony, however, and moved just as the point struck and broke off on his ribs. He started to scream now, and Skye eased into her moccasins and snatched up her tattered dress and disappeared into the forest.

She-Bear was waiting at the gnarled aspen about fifty yards from the camp. She held the rifle in her hand and a gun belt and holster with an Army Colt in the other. As soon as Skye got back into her dress, She-Bear slipped the gun belt over Skye's head and over her left shoulder, so the holster and pistol dropped just above her right hip within easy reach of her good arm. She-Bear already had the buffalo robe slung over her back, and she picked up her leather bag. "You lead," she said.

Skye moved out, heading due west. The chaotic sounds coming from the camp indicated that the barbarians had not yet organized a search party. She feared she had not killed Captain Quint. She had gone for the eye first, knowing that would disable him. Her chances for a kill on a torso thrust with her feeble weapon had been remote. She took some satisfaction that he would know what it was like to have only one of something that was supposed to be a pair. Perhaps, some woman would tell him someday that his eye was ugly and repugnant to her.

15

THE ROUTE TO the river was a downhill run, and Skye and She-Bear, despite an occasional stumble over the unstable, rocky terrain, reached the river bank in less than a half hour. It had been dry, and the snows from the previous winter had pretty well melted off, leaving the river running at a low depth. Still, the water raced swiftly, tumbling and sweeping over its stone-covered bed with a force that could easily topple man or horse trying to cross. Two light-weight women made an easier target for the turbulent waters. One misstep could launch the escapees on a wild and violent journey down a white-water chute that dropped over falls and crushed against canyon walls. Agonizing death awaited.

Skye jogged along the river bank, her eyes searching out a viable crossing point. She paused several times and studied promising passages before rejecting them. Finally, she came to a widening of the river that interested her. She stopped and turned to She-Bear. "This might work. What do you think?"

"It is a longer crossing."

"But it should be shallower . . . no higher than our waists at the deepest, I would think. And the water slows some here."

"Can we not just stay on this side of the river?"

"No, I think we must cross. They will search this side first, and they will have their own problems with crossing. They will also wonder if we were swept down the river. We have no choice."

She-Bear shrugged and nodded agreement, although Skye sensed that the younger woman had reservations. Obviously, the tough warrior-woman, who could cut a man's throat without flinching, did not have a fondness for water. Skye, in sharp contrast, was very much at home in water. She had yet to judge, however, how much her missing forearm would handicap her movement there. Once again, Skye shed her moccasins and garments. Then she retrieved some of the rawhide strips from She-Bear's bag and with her single hand, with which she was becoming increasingly dexterous, bound everything into a bundle and tied it around her, so it fit snugly under her chin. She-Bear watched and followed suit.

When their clothing was secure, the women each had a bulky, but not terribly heavy, load. Skye kept the holstered Colt slung over her shoulder, and She-Bear carried her rifle and the deerskin bag in one hand and the buffalo robe on her back. Skye did not know how to equalize the burden, for her single hand would be needed during the task of crossing the river.

Before they entered the icy water, Skye spoke to She-Bear. "You have been a brave young woman. We are going survive this. You must believe. You will take my hand as we cross the river. Do not let go. I will not let you. We travel this path together. We will do this."

Skye stepped into the river's edge, finding that the current swept only about her ankles. She commenced walking slowly toward the west bank, her feet, although numbing already from the frigid water, feeling the bite of each sharp stone. She-Bear gripped her hand like a vise as, step by careful step, they approached the river's center, the water climbing now to their upper thighs and its increased thrust threatening to knock them over. Suddenly, Skye felt a jolting yank on her arm, and she saw that She-Bear had lost her footing and was being pulled away by the water. In the moonlight she could see her friend's terror-filled eyes, and she planted her feet and held fast, while the younger woman struggled to regain her footing. She could feel her own feet slipping when the pressure on her arm eased, and she could see She-Bear had found a foothold and was moving slowly toward her.

When She-Bear had returned to her place beside her and they had taken a moment to regroup, Skye started the slow pace again, pleasantly surprised to find they had evidently forded the deepest of the river. She took heart now that each step brought them nearer the river's edge, and when they finally reached it, they both collapsed exhausted on the bank.

After a few minutes, however, Skye forced herself to her feet and nudged She-Bear to do the same. They dressed and quickly disappeared into the trees. No sooner had they done so than the sound of excited voices came from across the river. The barbarians had finally organized to give chase, but to Skye they seemed disorganized and confused. No person appeared to be in command of the hunt. She assumed the Captain was not yet able to resume command, but she knew that when he did, he would do so with a vengeance, and she would not underestimate his cunning. "We must go west away from the river," she said. "They will not decide we have crossed it for some time, and when they do, they will expect us to follow the river's course. We shall, but from several miles distant. We will go higher into the mountains where we can view the river below us and follow deer trails there. We will also be able to see if the barbarians have found our tracks."

"I understand, but we will need rest."

"We will travel at night when they cannot see us. We will sleep during the day." Skye turned toward the west and began to walk at a brisk pace, tossing a look over her shoulder to confirm that She-Bear followed. She did.

As the night wore on, their course led them to steeper ground. They paused for a rest. Skye studied the rocky landscape and spotted a deer trail leading higher into the mountains. "It is time to climb," she said.

Near dawn they stopped at a large outcropping of rock that jutted from the mountainside like a huge molar. It gave them a perfect viewing platform, yet, at its hollowed-out base, they were well protected from the sight of anyone in the river valley below. The climb had been steep, but Skye felt they needed to go no higher. From here on they would try to travel parallel to the river until they decided it was safe to cross again. Then they would descend from the mountainside.

They sat down in their rock-nest and ate some jerky and drank from the canteen they had filled from a stream they had found snaking its way down the mountainside toward the Powder River. Silently, She-Bear unbundled the buffalo robe and spread it on the ground. She lay down and quickly dropped off in a deep slumber. After a final survey of the valley below, Skye lay down beside her, pulled the edge of the robe over the two of them as far as it would reach, and submitted her own surrender to sleep.

They slept most of the morning, until Skye was awakened by the sound of distant voices. She started to nudge She-Bear but saw that her friend was awake and alert, having apparently heard the sounds, also. They climbed to the top of the outcropping and peered over. Perhaps a half hour's climb below, two men were following their trail.

"The Pawnee horse dung," She-Bear whispered.

"Yes, and it is too late to outrun them."

16

WHEN ETHAN AWOKE well before sunrise, he felt the firm pressure of something snuggled against his back. He sighed. Running Fox must have moved his robe after Ethan finished his watch. The boy had kept his distance after their unpleasantness yesterday, but, like a young puppy, he had returned, all the scolding forgotten. Ethan slipped out of his bedroll and reached for his moccasins. He saw that McLarty's buffalo robe had already been rolled up and secured, and there was no sign of the man anywhere. He could make out the shadowy outline of Jeb in the trees near the edge of camp. It was deathly quiet out there, it occurred to him. Usually, by this time the birds would be starting their morning chorus.

He got up and fastened his gun belt and retrieved the Winchester which lay next to his bedroll. Then he strolled over to check in with Jeb. "Somebody's out there, aren't they?"

"Can't see them. But, yep, they're here."

"Where's One Ball?"

"Got up two hours ago, right after I relieved you. Disappeared like a damn ghost. The old fart's kind of creepy, if you ask me."

"Yeah, but I'm glad we took him on. He knows this country, and he knows Indians. He may save our scalps."

"Puma." The gruff voice came from the south near the trail that ran along the riverbank.

"I hear you," Ethan called back. "Show yourself."

"Peace?"

"Yes, we want no trouble."

He felt a tugging on his shirt. "That Badger Claw. From my people."

"I know Badger Claw." He did not add that he and the warrior had an uneasy relationship. The Brule coveted Skye and pressed to take her as a second or third wife. She had made it clear that she would be a man's only wife—if she chose to have a man at all. Still, Badger Claw seemed to view Ethan as a rival. On the other hand, Ethan conceded he owed the man his life, because the Brule warrior had appeared with some of his tribesmen at a moment of crisis to take down some men who would surely have killed Skye and himself.

Momentarily, Badger Claw appeared on the trail, leading his spotted horse and trailed by two other warriors and their ponies. He was a man of small stature and a handsome warrior with erect bearing, broad shoulders and sinewy muscles that sheathed the naked arms extending from his vested torso. Ethan knew he was a respected warrior and a sub-chief of some sort. Because of Lame Buffalo's death, it was not difficult to see this warrior assuming leadership of the remnants of the band. It was difficult to guess what direction he might lead.

Ethan waved the visitors into the camp, and they came warily. Badger Claw's eyes searched the site, and he spoke something in Lakota to Running Fox, who had never left Ethan's side. Running Fox translated, "Him say you not have many warriors for war party."

"I thought he spoke English."

"Not many words. No speak good English like me do."

"Tell him he does not have many warriors either, but we know there are more with him . . . at least three others." Ethan was gambling that McLarty had been on target with his estimate.

Running Fox repeated the message, and Badger Claw could not hide his surprise.

"Here's the rest of the so-called war party."

Ethan turned to find McLarty walking out of the pines with his Sharps pointed at the backs of three grim-faced Sioux warriors, who had clearly been disarmed and were now humiliated in the presence of their leader. McLarty's face was expressionless. "Shall I put 'em out of their misery?"

"No, we just need to keep them in front of us. Let's invite them to share breakfast and see what we can find out. Do you speak some Lakota?"

"Some. Just enough to get by. Sounds like the papoose was doing okay. Let him do the talking. Maybe he'll turn out to be good for something."

"Running Fox, invite them to join us at our fire and share our breakfast. We'll talk."

Badger Claw grunted his acceptance, and an hour later, after studying the fare suspiciously, the guests ate voraciously of Jeb's hotcakes, saturated with the last of the maple syrup. They smacked noisily, as they licked and sucked their fingers clean of the sticky mess that had resulted absent the use of forks, which were foreign to them.

While they ate, Ethan learned that Badger Claw and his warriors had been part of the Brule hunting party that had returned to the destroyed village. Most of the hunters had taken the meager meat harvest from the hunt and commenced trailing the exodus from the village. Badger Claw and his warriors had taken on the task of tracking the raiders, not knowing what they might find.

Ethan with the help of his young interpreter told the visitors what they knew about the attack on the village and explained that the survivors of the raid had been moved to Ethan's ranch, which did not seem to set well with Badger Claw. Running Fox also informed the warrior that his wife had been killed in the raid, but his six-year old son survived. The news was accepted stoically, but Ethan supposed the man had been prepared for such a report and, perhaps, was grateful to have salvaged his son.

Ethan suggested the two groups join forces, but Badger Claw rejected the idea immediately. He refused to be slowed by the white eyes, and they would only be in his way, he insisted. Besides, he knew of the man called One Ball. He was not to be trusted. Ethan had a hunch that the humiliation inflicted by McLarty's capture of Badger Claw's comrades factored into the warrior's opinion of the old mountain man.

"We will be following you. If you wish our help, you have only to ask," Ethan said. He decided that the Sioux might be better trackers on this cold trail, so it did not matter if he allowed them to move ahead. Ethan would not be far behind. When the fighting came, they would be shooting at the same enemy.

When Badger Claw and his warriors had collected the weapons McLarty had forced them to abandon in the forest, they rode out of the campsite, taking the trail north that followed the Powder River. It occurred to Ethan that the raiders had never deviated from the river's course, and they clearly were not moving at random. They were headed for a predetermined destination. But where?

Running Fox stood beside him as they watched the Sioux ride off. "Me help?" the boy asked.

Ethan tousled the boy's hair. "Yes, you helped." He had to concede that Running Fox's availability as an interpreter had assisted hugely, although he suspected McLarty was no stranger to the language. For some reason the old man had remained silent during the conversation with their guests, but he had listened and watched with narrowed eyes.

"Badger Claw take Sky-in-the-Morning for his woman."

The remark grabbed Ethan's attention. "Why do you say that?"

"Him say she no be second woman. Now she would be first woman. That why Badger Claw not want us to slow him."

It had not occurred to Ethan that he had a rival. Surely Skye would not be attracted to this warrior, although he had to admit that the man struck a striking physical presence. He had trouble seeing Skye living out her life in a Sioux village or on a reservation, although she had a definite altruistic side and had taught at the Quaker school for several years. Perhaps she would find a life in the service of her people a persuasive call. And what better way than to marry a warrior and truly share their lives?

He found that the whole notion annoyed him and scolded himself that such thoughts were foolish, since he did not even know if Skye was alive.

McLarty was leading his horse over to his saddle, which lay near the dying embers of the fire. "I didn't sign up for this party to spend the days on my ass. If you don't mind, I'd like to move on and get whatever we're going to do over and done with."

Ethan couldn't argue with that thought. "We'll pull out in the next fifteen minutes."

"And we won't take the river trail," McLarty said softly, but with a firmness in his voice.

Ethan considered the man's remark. It made sense. If the raiders were traveling the broken Powder River Trail, they likely expected pursuit and were prepared for it. McLarty knew this country. It would make sense to listen to him, even at the risk of losing more time. "You can take the lead. We'll follow."

As they rode out, Jeb sidled his horse up next to Ethan. "The boy was a big help as an interpreter. Somehow, I just didn't trust McLarty to pass on the words the way you said them."

"What do you know about the Sioux language?"

"Absolutely nothing."

"There are actually three Sioux dialects. The Sioux are spread out across the northern plains . . . from here and north into Canada and east into Minnesota. There are three divisions based primarily on language. The westernmost are Lakota, and they're made up of seven sub-tribes, including the Brule, Oglala and Hunkpapa . . . that's Sitting Bull's bunch. These sub-tribes all speak Lakota. They make up kind of a confederation, sometimes called the seven council fires."

"Sounds complicated."

"Some of the sub-tribes have negotiated their separate peace with the white man. But they're all family. And since the treaties are always broken, you can't count on where they'll line up if war breaks out. The Black Hills are sacred to the Lakota, and the Fort Laramie Treaty of 1868 prohibited white settlement forever. When gold was discovered there four years back, that treaty went to hell. That's what started the current fuss."

"Sounds like something we want to stay away from."

"Yeah, I'd say so."

17

SKYE DECIDED IMMEDIATELY that they would be no match for the Pawnee in hand-to-hand combat. She told She-Bear to take her Winchester and move up the slope some twenty yards into a cluster of pine and aspen that cloaked a patch of the mountainside. She calculated that the outcropping that provided their hideaway should block the Pawnees' line of sight, as the young woman scurried away.

Before she left, Skye asked She-Bear, "Can you hit a man from that distance?"

"I believe I can do this."

"Do not shoot until you hear my pistol fire."

"I understand."

As She-Bear worked her way up the incline, Skye pulled the Army Colt from its holster and studied it. She had some knowledge of pistols from observation but had never fired one. All the chambers of the cylinder were loaded. She held the gun in her hand and raised it as if to fire. She found the weapon was heavier than she realized, and her hand shook noticeably. Nothing she could do about it. She sat down on the buffalo robe and tugged it around her, covering any evidence of the gun. Then she waited, her hand gripping the pistol tightly and rubbing her fingers over it, attempting to get acquainted.

The wait could not have been more than fifteen minutes, but it seemed like an hour. The voices had faded to silence, but she could hear the rattle of loose rock rolling away as the Pawnee crept up the mountainside. Abruptly, a squatty, barrel-chested man stepped around the edge of the outcropping. At first, he appeared startled to find her there, and then their eyes met, and his mouth contorted into a scowl. His hand lifted the war axe he carried at his side and he moved threateningly toward her as his taller companion emerged from behind the rock and edged next to him. The second Pawnee said something to the other, and, although Skye could not understand the words, the two men cast their eyes about uneasily, and she suspected they were wondering about the whereabouts of She-Bear.

The squatty warrior stood no more than a dozen feet from her now and began waving the axe wildly and screaming at her. She gathered he was instructing her to get up. She flipped back the robe and aimed the pistol, which was quivering in her hand. She squeezed the trigger, resulting in a deafening explosion, and the gun almost kicked from her hand. The Indians both leaped back, and she realized her shot had missed. The Pawnee charged her like an angry bull, and, for some reason, the weapon steadied now. She heard another shot, and a second, before she fired again. This time, the bullet tore into his throat before she sent another into his chest, and he collapsed on her legs.

She swung the Colt around, seeking the other Pawnee, and then she saw him crumpled on the ground, his head an island in a pool of blood. She pushed the dead Pawnee off her legs and scrambled up. She turned and caught sight of She-Bear, half-running and half-sliding down the rocky slope, with a rare smile on her face. When she reached the outcropping, she went directly to the side of the warrior her rifle shots had taken down. She knelt, and her fingers latched the man's hair and lifted his head. She looked up at Skye and displayed two fingers. "Both shots hit. Did I not tell you I could do this?"

"You did. Your shooting was amazing. And I missed my first shot from ten feet away." Then Skye saw that She-Bear was not listening. She had drawn her skinning knife from its sheath and was focused on removing her dead target's scalp. Skye's stomach was suddenly queasy. "What are you doing?"

"I am taking my first scalp."

"Why, for God's sake?"

"Why not? Our warriors take the scalps of fallen enemies. I think after the things we have done, I am a warrior now, too. This is my second kill and it did not occur to me to take the white sentry's scalp. The scalp of a hated Pawnee is a special prize, though. You should take your kill's scalp."

"No, I think not."

"It will be wasted then. I cannot take the scalp of an enemy I did not kill." She lifted the blood-dripping scalp from the dead man and draped it over a boulder to dry.

"We need to drag the bodies away from here, but first we take their clothes."

"Their clothes? Why?"

"Do you want to keep wearing what remains of our dresses through the brush and brambles? We can wash their things in the stream and get some of the dirt and stink out. They will be warmer and offer more protection to our bodies." She looked over the two dead men. She-Bear's kill was taller and wore faded denim britches and a flannel shirt with a buckskin vest, and the Pawnee she had shot was attired in buckskin pants and a bloody war shirt pocked with several bullet holes. "You take your kill's things, and I will remove these. From far away Quint's killers might not recognize us. We can use your rawhide strips to draw up the waists and cut anything else down that's too long."

When the Pawnee were stripped, She-Bear nodded at the Pawnee she called her kill. "This one mounted me," she said. "His spear has shriveled to a tiny grub. It is fitting. I think I should remove it that he might walk the spirit world without it."

"No," Skye said, "you have done enough."

In a short time, each pulling an arm, they drug the naked Pawnee corpses away from their hideaway behind the outcropping to a rock ledge that stuck out over a small canyon. They rolled the bodies off and watched them drop like dying birds through the air to the canyon floor. Then they washed the pirated clothing in the stream, rubbing the garments over the stones repeatedly and then scraping them with pine bark before laying them out to dry on boulders that surrounded their hiding place.

When the tasks were completed they settled back into what Skye had come to think of as their "nest" in the rocks. They both eased down on the buffalo robe and slept for the better part of an hour. When she awakened, Skye spoke. "I think we should stay where we are for a day, perhaps two."

"But what if someone heard our guns. Will they not come this way?"

"I do not think anyone could tell that closely where the shots came from. Even if someone did, they would likely think the Pawnee had killed us, and they would await a report from the warriors we killed. It is more likely most of the searchers remain on the other side of the river, and, regardless, they probably did not expect us to stray this far from the river. They will likely be searching south until they give up the hunt."

"But how will we know?"

"In a day or two we will go back the way we came and see if they are still camped across the river. If so, we will then start our journey south. If they have left, we will cross again and take the main trail on the other side of the river. I believe some of our people will be searching for us or, at least, following the vengeance trail."

"What makes you think Captain Quint will leave the camp?"

"He was planning to leave before we escaped. He is searching for gold he believes to be at a trading post my father once kept for the Cheyenne and other tribes. He did not say as much, but I believe he knows how to find the post, and that is where he is headed. He thought I knew where the gold was hidden there. If he decides we have escaped, he will not want to tarry here. He is not a stupid man, and he will be aware of the possibility of a war party following him. Unless he is dying, he will move soon."

"If we are to stay here, we must find something to eat."

"We will starve if you wait for me to kill an animal with my pistol. I suggest you go hunting, while I search out some roots and dried berries for a meal."

"I will find a rabbit or a squirrel."

18

I T HAD BEEN two days since Ethan's little party had met up with Badger Claw and his band of warriors. One Ball McLarty had led them single-file on a spiderweb of narrow deer paths through the forested mountains. Somehow, Ethan conceded, the old mountain man always sensed which branch in the maze of trails to take and kept the group parallel to the Powder River which was about a mile to the west. Because of McLarty's keen instincts, they had likely lost little time in taking this route instead of the river trail.

It was nearly dusk, and they reined in the horses when they came to a patch of scrub trees and seedlings that could be quickly cleared for a cold camp. As they dismounted, Ethan directed a question to McLarty. "We'll need to connect up with the river trail when we catch up with the raiders, I suspect. How do we know when to change course?"

"I'll tell you," McLarty said softly.

It was pointless to pursue the question further. McLarty rarely spoke, and Ethan had learned the man had little interest in conversation. So far, he had no reason to distrust McLarty, and he would not press.

They broke out some more hardtack and beef jerky, and Ethan found himself remembering why he did not miss his scouting days. The diet was becoming monotonous.

They laid out their bedrolls. Running Fox spread his buffalo robe next to Ethan's spot, and Ethan did not protest. The boy had travelled without complaint and did more than his share of camp chores. Ethan knew he was a bright boy, and probably understood now that he should not have followed, and, accordingly, was determined not to be a problem.

Everyone but One Ball McLarty curled up in their bedrolls. He sat on the ground, leaning against a tree trunk, a wool blanket wrapped about his shoulders and his head resting on his chest. Ethan had noticed the man often slept the entire night in that position—assuming he ever slept. Regardless, he had decided that posting a watch was unnecessary with McLarty in camp.

It was nearly two o'clock in the morning when Ethan was awakened by the sound of distant gunfire. He sat up and pushed his blanket aside. He looked about the campsite and saw that McLarty had lifted his head but had not otherwise changed positions. Jeb was stirring and tossing his blankets aside. Jeb spoke softly, "Trouble for somebody."

"Your Indian friends, I'd guess," McLarty replied.

"The shots are in the direction of the river," Jeb said.

"Badger Claw and his outfit just made their acquaintance with the varmints we're tracking," McLarty said.

"Shouldn't we go help?" Jeb asked.

"Too late for that by the time we'd get there," McLarty said. "I'm going to get some more shuteye. I'll take a look over that way at sunrise."

McLarty closed his eyes and his chin dropped to his chest again. End of conversation. Ethan looked at Jeb. "I'm wanting to check this out, but One Ball's right. There's nothing to be done right now." He lay back down and listened until the gunfire became sporadic about fifteen minutes later and, in another fifteen minutes, ceased altogether. His mind resisted sleep as it ran through the different scenarios that might be playing out along the river trail, but finally he drifted off.

When he awakened, Ethan saw that McLarty had disappeared. He guessed that the old mountain man had left to check out the early morning disturbance. They were not all that far from whatever hostilities had broken out, so there would be no fire this morning. He would ferret out whatever he could find of the jerky and crumbling biscuits for breakfast, but he was ready to have Jeb put together a real meal soon.

Jeb got up and joined him, but he decided to let Running Fox sleep until McLarty returned. "Did you hear One Ball slip out of camp?" Ethan asked.

"Hell, no. I can't hear him move around when I'm wide awake. He's a creepy old bastard, but I've got to admit I sleep better with him around."

"I won't argue with that. I'm afraid I'm getting a little lazy about watching out for trouble. I know my eyes and ears aren't up to his standards."

"I'm curious as hell to know what he finds over by the river."

Several hours later McLarty returned. He walked into camp without saying a word and started helping himself to the scraps that comprised breakfast. Then, he reclaimed his tree and sat down to eat. Ethan knew that the old man was playing a game of some kind, waiting for someone to ask. He surrendered. "What did you find?"

"Like I said, your Indians found some trouble. Four dead, one dying, and the other wounded. The one you called 'Badger Claw' will probably make it. That's the way it works. He led the fools into the ambush, and he gets out alive. Ain't never no justice."

"Where is he now?"

"Gathering up their horses and waiting to send his friend off to the Happy Hunting Ground. I said he could wait for us or go on by hisself. Didn't make us no matter. I'd bet he waits."

"What about the men that ambushed them?" Jeb asked.

"Well, Mr. Oaks, they've moved on up the trail. They had a big camp over by the river. Fifteen or so men, I'd say. Not counting the three or four women. Got to be the friends you're after. They was smart enough to keep the trail guarded, and I'd guess they had plenty of warning about their Indian visitors. They was pretty much packed to move up the trail this morning, I'd guess. When the fools parade showed up, they took care of them and decided to get on their way."

"I'd like to see the camp near the Powder," Ethan said. "And we need to see what Badger Claw has in mind. We could use another fighting man, if he'll follow orders."

"You can follow my trail back to the river. Then you can stay on the river trail for a spell. I'll try to scout east of the trail through the woods and see what they've got for lookouts. Kill one or two, if need be. Odds are they're not thinking much about a second batch of fools this soon. And they're not just on the run. They know more or less where they're headed."

"But they're going deeper into Cheyenne country, and they haven't been too friendly lately."

"Not just the Cheyenne. The Sioux and other tribes up this way have got something brewing, and they ain't fussing much with each other right now. These folks ain't up here for a damned vacation."

19

AFTER MCLARTY DISAPPEARED into the trees, Ethan rousted Running Fox out of his robe, and they followed the mountain man's tracks back to the river, where they found a subdued Badger Claw wedging his dead companions into the lower branches of trees along the river. The top of the warrior's scalp was matted with blood, some drying, but scarlet still leaked from a wound. Ethan vowed to examine it when the Sioux was finished with whatever he was doing with the bodies, which were now five. He had asked the boy to talk to Badger Claw and see what he could learn of the man's injury and find out what he was doing. Running Fox had seemed pleased to have an assignment and linked up with his fellow tribesman immediately, helping with the placement of the corpses when needed. It seemed a macabre task for a small boy, but he supposed this was nothing in comparison to what the boy had dealt with in his ravaged village.

Ethan and Jeb studied the abandoned campsite while Badger Claw and Running Fox attended to the placement of the bodies. Jeb wandered off to the camp's edge and shortly called to Ethan. "Come take a look at this, Boss."

Ethan joined him in a little clearing set off from the camp and found the cowhand standing next to the charred remains of a fire. The ground was pretty much devoid of vegetation, and the sparse grass that did exist was flattened, obviously by sleeping occupants. He noticed immediately the small moccasin tracks that were scattered about the area. "This must be where they kept the women. Or at least they spent time here."

"That's what I figured. They . . . or some of them . . . were still alive while they were here."

Ethan circled the clearing and found a break in the brush. He stopped and pushed his way past the barbed gooseberry bushes that were on both sides of the opening. He returned quickly, wrinkling his nose.

"What's the matter, Boss?"

"Above ground latrine." He continued his perusal of the clearing fringes until he paused at a narrower opening and again stepped into the woods. "I'm going to see where this goes. Why don't you and Running Fox see if you can catch a few fish, and we'll stick around here for some dinner."

"No argument from me. About time for some fresh biscuits, too."

As Chief of Scouts at Fort Laramie, tracking had been Ethan's strong suit, and he saw something that interested him. A lone woman's moccasin-clad feet left prints angling into the forest. Broken pine sprigs and flattened blades of grass leading deeper into the woods intrigued him more. A captive would not likely have been permitted to wander this far from camp, and the woman seemed to be moving fast, making no effort to hide her tracks. He followed the woman's trail until he came to a tall gnarled aspen, where it was obvious another woman had joined her. The two had then swung west toward the river. This showed no indication of being an authorized journey. There was no evidence of pursuit, so any search must have been disorganized. He wondered if there was a distraction of some kind.

It took no special skill to track the women to the river's edge, but the trail stopped abruptly there. He did find other, larger moccasin tracks along the river bank—two men, it appeared. He remembered Otter had mentioned that several Pawnee rode with the raiders. The women were without doubt on the run, and they had either crossed the Powder or been swept away by it. He could find no signs of a struggle, so the pursuers had not captured them here. The river was wide at this point and appeared to run shallow. He took off his own moccasins and waded into the water. The rush of the river was strong against his legs, but he stepped cautiously and found the footing solid.

When he stepped up on the other bank, Ethan quickly picked up the trail. The women had crossed the Powder, but there was no doubt that the Pawnee were still on the hunt. This triggered a sinking feeling in his gut. There was no way the women would outrun the Pawnee. He began to move ahead at a trot, following the tracks and other signs that left a virtual map for a man of his experience.

Three hours later the trees started to thin out and the incline turned noticeably steeper. The mountain slopes in front of him promised a more serious climb, and all the tracks and loose rock indicated both duos had angled toward a good-sized stone outcropping on much higher terrain. He studied the mountainside above him. Some hundred feet south of the rock formation, he saw the black, shadowy vultures circling and swooping—dozens of them. The sight was nothing but ominous, and he steeled himself for the worst as he commenced his ascent.

Suddenly, a rifle cracked twice, kicking up rocks at his feet, and he dived and rolled downhill, coming up near a clump of aspen with his rifle ready. He was certain the shots came from near the outcropping which was a logical sniper's nest. But why would someone be hiding in that place? There would be no reason for anyone to be expecting him. If the Pawnee had captured the women, they had either returned them to the camp via another route or killed them, which he feared was the case. They would not be holed up behind the rocks. This left him baffled. Surely one of the women had not fired the rifle. If so, she knew how to handle the damn thing.

He had decent cover in the trees, but he couldn't leave the spot without giving the shooter a tempting target. The rifleman could escape in the opposite direction but, certainly, was not going to come Ethan's direction without exposure to his own fire. It was pretty much a standoff for now. The night was his friend, however, for that was when the puma stalked. And darkness would descend on the mountains in a few hours.

Ethan waited, studying the lay of the land and planning a route up the slope. He would need to work his way south, so he did not attempt his assent in the line of fire.

His thought was to inch up the mountainside and come in behind the shooter. If the Pawnee were ensconced in the rock, Ethan had to keep an eye out, for it was possible one of the warriors might take a notion to sneak away with the thought of taking the attack to him.

As the shadows began to cover the mountains, Ethan slowly and silently eased his way down the slope, disappearing into the more heavily forested zone. Under cover of both trees and darkness, he slipped quickly through the woods at the mountain's base until he felt he was out of sight to anyone hidden in the rocks. Then, clinging to his rifle and staying in the shadows and close to the ground, he began to work snail-like up the incline.

It took him nearly two hours to finally get a bit higher than the outcropping and some fifty yards to the south. He had a clear view of the objective and in the moonlight that streaked through cloud cover could make out the outline of someone standing with a rifle at the far end of the rock escarpment. His long hair fell over his shoulders, and Ethan figured the rifleman had to be one of the Pawnee. But where was the other? He was positioned to assure a clean shot with his rifle. Still, he felt he needed to verify his enemy before taking the man down. With his Winchester ready to fire at the squeeze of the trigger and belly to the ground, Ethan began crawling toward the rifleman.

When he was within nearly twenty paces, he stood and aimed. "Drop your weapon and turn around," he commanded. He hoped the Pawnee spoke some English.

The rifle clattered to the ground and the figure turned toward him. In the same instant, out of the corner of his eye he caught movement and turned his head to see someone racing toward him with a skinning knife in hand. Just as the attacker was within reach, Ethan swung the barrel of his rifle down and hammered it against the side of the man's head. The attacker dropped like a sack of corn and the knife fell away. He instantly whirled to face the other party, who was reaching for the rifle. "Don't even think about it," he yelled, "or you're dead."

He moved closer to the shadowy figure. The Pawnee evidently understood some English, or he would be dead. "Where are the women?" he asked.

"Why do you ask that? We are the women. Who are you? I do not recognize you?"

A woman's voice. What in the hell? "My name is Ethan Ramsey. Who are you?"

"I am called She-Bear. And I have seen you in our village with Sky-in-the-Morning."

"My God. I almost shot you. Where is Skye?"

She-Bear raced past him. "Behind you. She is the one you struck with your rifle."

"No," he uttered in disbelief. "But she tried to kill me. I thought you were both Pawnee."

"And we thought you were one of the barbarians who slaughtered our people."

They both knelt beside Skye, who was flattened on her back, stirring in a futile effort to turn over, and moaning loudly. Thank God. At least, he had not killed her. His fingers pushed the hair away from her face, and he was stunned by what he saw there. The rifle barrel had struck her above the left eye and left a bloody mass that covered her forehead. But the right side of her face was also swollen with raw wounds that appeared they might have resulted from savage raking by a grizzly bear's claws.

"It's turning cold. We need to get her near a fire where she can get some warmth and where we can look at her wound."

She-Bear pointed at a pocket behind some boulders. "Our buffalo robe is over there, and a fire pit is nearby. There should be coals underneath the ashes. I can start a fire, but we have been afraid to let one burn at night, because it might lead someone to our hiding place."

"The barbarians, as you call them, are gone. We have made camp there, and you are safe now. It would be good if my friends saw a fire. It might reassure them of my own safety."

He lifted Skye from the ground, and, although she flailed helplessly, he easily carried her to the robe and placed her on it, thinking that the five and one-half foot woman must weigh less than a hundred pounds. While She-Bear stirred the hot coals and tossed tinder in the shallow fire pit, Ethan pulled a kerchief from his coat pocket and retrieved the canteen he spotted among the fugitives' scant gear. He sat down beside Skye and began to wipe the blood from the flesh about her eye, which was already nearly swollen shut. An enormous knot had erupted on her brow above the eye. A cut there seemed to be the source of the bleeding, but it did not seem terribly deep.

He spoke softly to her as he cleaned her face. "Skye, can you hear me? It's Ethan. Everything is going to be fine now."

Her good eye fluttered and then opened. She seemed to be taking in her surroundings. He continued to assure her of her safety, telling her repeatedly who he was. She remained silent for some minutes before she spoke groggily. "Ethan, what are you doing here?"

"I have been looking for you. Thank God, I found you."

"What happened to me?"

How did he explain this? "It's my fault. I hit you with my rifle barrel."

She seemed to be trying to make sense of his answer. "Why would you hit me?"

"I thought you were someone else . . . one of the Pawnee."

Again, she did not respond for some time. Then she finally spoke. "I tried to kill you, didn't I?"

"Yes, and I'm happy to report you were not successful. But I'm sorry I hurt you."

"This is all very confusing, and I am tired."

"Everything's fine. Go to sleep. We'll talk in the morning."

Her eyes closed and she drifted off quickly. The fire's flames were delivering warmth his way, and he looked at the flickering blaze and, through the smoke, saw She-Bear staring back at him, studying him with dark, intelligent eyes. He flipped part of the robe to cover Skye and scooted nearer to the fire. He returned the young woman's gaze and it struck him that she was younger than he first thought, probably no more than seventeen or eighteen. And the dust and sweat of days on the trail could not hide that she was quite attractive. He had noticed that she was tall for her people, male or female, likely five feet and nine or ten inches.

She was obviously fluent in his language, thankfully, so he decided to satisfy his curiosity. "Can we speak now?" he asked.

"Yes, I have questions."

He thought he was going to be asking the questions. "Very well. You first."

"How did you come to be here?"

He gave her a brief version of his story, explaining his arrival at the village and the moving of her people to his ranch and finishing with the ambush of Badger Claw's Sioux warriors on the trail. "I found signs of your escape and followed you here. I also discovered the Pawnee tracks, and I feared you were dead. I did not know Skye had escaped the camp, but I suspected."

"We killed the Pawnee." She plucked the scalp from her crude belt and held it up. "We each had a kill. I took a scalp. Sky-in-the-Morning would not do so." She described the trap they laid for the Pawnee pursuers in detail and with evident pride. "Sky-in-the-Morning is very brave, but you would not have been in any danger if she had tried to shoot you this night. You must teach her to use the gun."

"I'll do that if she will allow me. You apparently need no help with your rifle."

"No, you are alive because I did not recognize you and chose only to warn with my shots."

"Thank you for that kindness. Now, I could use a few hours' sleep. Why don't you share the robe with Skye? I can curl up here near the fire and keep it going."

"Do you not wish to share the robe with her after making this journey?"

Her question flustered him for a few moments. "Uh, no, I do not think she would appreciate that."

"But you would be willing," she said with a knowing smile. "I do not think you traveled these many miles to rescue me."

Ethan tugged his coat collar up about his neck and stretched out near the fire. "I'm going to get some shut-eye."

20

SKYE SAT ON the buffalo robe watching Ethan as he slept near the fire. The sun had already crawled over the mountain peaks and nearly blinded the only eye that was working. At least, unlike Captain Quint, her disabled eye would function soon. It was difficult to pinpoint a place her head did not hurt. She could feel the massive lump above her eye, and the stabbing pain seemed to shoot out in all directions from there. And then the side of her face that had taken the blows of the quirt had seemed to swell more and bring renewed agony. She feared infection that would leave scarring that would turn her into a one-armed witch woman. But she was alive, she reminded herself.

She-Bear had risen with the sun and replenished the fire and was now roasting what remained of a rabbit she had killed yesterday. Skye had tried to get up with her but dizziness and vertigo struck and plopped her back down on the robe. Ethan woke up and lifted himself from the ground. He seemed unperturbed by his rocky mattress, but she supposed he had endured such accommodations many times during his years as an Army Scout. He cast a look her way, apparently checking her condition. Then he walked away from their nest, she suspected to relieve himself.

When he returned, he moved toward the robe and stood above her. "I wish I could say you looked better, but the sunlight doesn't help. How do you feel?"

"Thank you for the compliment. You have looked better yourself. A shave and a bath might help, but I'm not certain. As to how I feel, I guess better than one might expect after being nearly clubbed to death. But outside of an unrelenting headache, dizziness is my main issue. I can't seem to stand up without falling over. I'm sure that will pass."

"Well, we can't stay here. We need to leave this morning. Everybody is going to wonder what happened to me. I'd like to be at camp by mid-afternoon."

"Who is 'everybody'?"

"That would be my cowhand, Jeb Oaks, my small friend, Running Fox, and Badger Claw. At some point, One Ball McLarty will turn up."

"You make no sense. Running Fox, Badger Claw, and someone named One Ball? This is a rescue party?"

"Best I could come up with. I've told She-Bear the story. She can fill you in." He turned away and approached the fire.

She-Bear had finished roasting the rabbit and cut off a hind quarter and some ribs and handed it to him, and the remainder she took to the robe and sat down next to Skye and began parceling out the rest of the meat. Ethan stood next to the fire and chewed the meat off the bones, depositing the remnants in the fire as he cleaned the meat off.

Skye thought he looked rather uncouth as he stood there gnawing on the bones, but then she considered they were not dining in a fancy hotel ballroom. She admitted she was annoyed with the man this morning. She was angry because he had hit her with the rifle barrel, although she knew her reaction was irrational. She guessed most folks being charged by someone brandishing a skinning knife would not sit still and wait for the blade to start carving. But then he had just walked into the nest and taken charge and slept late to boot. She could not resist needling him. "The Puma has become lazy it appears, sleeping in his den while the woman gets up and cares for the fire and prepares breakfast. Someone could have murdered us all while we slept."

He gave her a look that indicated she had struck a raw spot. "I would have heard if a stranger approached. I can sense those things."

"Well, don't think we are going to become slaves for the camp chores and cooking when we join your little party."

"That's the furthest thought from my mind. But don't expect to be treated like a queen, either. Frankly, I don't know what we're going to do with you. She-Bear said the other women were alive when you escaped."

"Yes. They were afraid to come with us."

"Then we've got to try to help them. I'll probably send the two of you back to my ranch with Running Fox and Badger Claw, and Jeb and I will connect up with McLarty and continue tracking that bunch."

His words infuriated her. "You are not sending us anyplace, mister. We're going with you, and you had better get used to that idea right now."

"You'll just hold us up. You're in no condition to be chasing after a gang of killers."

"Allow me a day, and I will be ready to walk or ride. As for the killers, I think we have already shown we can do our part. We have taken down two more barbarians than your so-called rescuers have killed so far . . . and we escaped without any help from you. The only things I have received from you is a knot on my head and a closed eye."

Ethan said nothing and began kicking dirt and rocks in the fire pit. He picked up the canteen and headed to the stream to fill it. She-Bear stood and began gathering up their weapons before she returned to the robe. "You and the Puma are like mountain cats in breeding season," she remarked, "you have to fight and fuss before you mate."

"That is a terrible thing to say."

She-Bear ignored her reply and helped Skye off the robe, leading her to the stone wall of the escarpment where she could lean and try to get her bearings. Skye watched while She-Bear rolled the buffalo robe into a tight bundle, but the dizziness returned, and she found herself slipping down the side of the stone wall and landing on her butt. Ethan returned with the canteen and walked over to her, his face grim. "You're not going to be able to walk back."

"If you can allow me another day, I am certain I will be fine."

"I can't do that. We've got a few medical supplies in my saddle bags at camp, and, with all due respect, your face needs some work."

"I guess you can shoot me and leave me for the vultures," she said sarcastically.

"Not this time." He turned to She-Bear. "Can you carry all the guns and gear?"

"Yes, I can do that."

"I'm going to help Skye down the mountain slope, and when we get to level ground, I'll carry her. She can ride my back."

"You cannot do that," Skye said. "I would feel like a fool, and I am too much of a load."

"It doesn't matter how you feel right now, and you're light as a feather. I weigh twice what you do. We'll be fine." He reached down and grasped her hand and pulled her up, and supporting her with his arm wrapped around her waist, they stepped out from behind the escarpment and started down the steep incline. He half carried her part of the trek, and at other times, she slid on the loose rock. She refused to give him the satisfaction of hearing her complain, but she couldn't help wincing when a sharp stone gouged her from time to time.

Ethan commented wryly, "We'll need to apply some horse liniment to your sore fanny when we get to camp."

She did not appreciate his sense of humor. "You won't be getting within ten feet of my fanny once we get out of here."

When they finally reached level ground, they rested and passed the canteen back and forth. "Save half," Ethan admonished. "We'll be moving mostly in shade, and it's cool enough one more stop should be good before we get to camp."

Too soon, Ethan got up. He helped her off the ground again and let her stand a few minutes. "Can you walk?"

She was determined that she would and took off in the lead. After a dozen steps, her head began to spin, and she collapsed to her knees. Ethan moved in front of her and waited a few moments.

"She-Bear, you'll need to help get her on my back."

It was one of those moments that Skye was acutely aware of her missing lower arm. An extra hand would have made the climb relatively easy, but she had trouble latching onto a solid anchor. Finally she positioned herself with her legs locked around Ethan's waist and her good right arm latched around his neck and her other upper arm locked under his chin. Her face rested against the side of his head. Once settled in, she found she was not that uncomfortable, and she would never tell the man, but she decided it was rather pleasant to be nestled close to him like this. She felt the tension slipping from her body for the first time in weeks.

He walked at a steady pace on the trail Skye and She-Bear had first broken through the forest. They stopped at least three times to rest before sharing the remaining water. She could see that Ethan was tiring and she felt guilty that she was causing this burden. She had tried walking on her own for a spell after each halt and was encouraged that she held out longer each time, but she admitted she would never have made the trek on her own. As they travelled on what she hoped was the last leg of their journey, she thought about how to handle the matter of Quint's search for the gold. It suddenly struck her for the first time that her people had been killed, raped, and maimed because of the gold. The barbarians had been searching for her as a route to the gold. If she had not been in the village, her band would not have been attacked. This was a terrible burden, and she wondered how she would come to terms with the guilt. She clutched Ethan a little tighter.

She heard the roaring of the river tumbling over the rocks before she saw it, and she sighed with relief that the trip was nearly ended. When they came to the river bank, she released her grip on Ethan and slid off his back. He drew his Colt from its holster, raised the gun in the air and fired it three times. No more than fifteen minutes later, a tall, dark-complexioned man appeared on the other side of the river. He was soon joined by a boy she recognized as Running Fox, whom she remembered was Good Heart's son. He had been a pupil at the Quaker school for a brief time, and she had tutored him in English with a small group of other young children while she was at the village.

"Good to see you, Boss. Your young friend has been worried something fearsome. And I was getting a mite concerned about my pay."

"We need some help with the river. Skye is injured, and I don't think I can carry her and keep my balance in the current."

"I'll get my lariat. My rope should reach across this river. It's not exactly Texas-wide."

Jeb headed downstream and was gone in an instant, but Running Fox remained. "Puma," he called, "me afraid you not come back. Maybe bad people kill you."

"I am okay, and I found two of your friends. How is Badger Claw?"

"He be good. Jeb cut bullet from head. Much better now. Sleeps much."

Skye said, "You have something of a sorry crew, don't you?"

"I suppose you could say so. And we can't take much time to recuperate. We need to be on the trail in the morning, or we'll never catch up. I hope McLarty has located them."

"You don't need to fret about finding them."

"Why not?"

"I know where they're headed. I'm not sure how far it is, but they'll be stopping for a spell."

"How do you know?"

"Captain Quint as much as told me when he was demonstrating his quirt. It has something to do with gold. I will tell you about it later."

"I also know something about gold. I think we'd better share some information."

21

ETHAN LEANED AGAINST a fallen trunk at the edge of the clearing, his legs stretched out in front of him. He decided there wasn't a muscle in his body that didn't ache, and his back and shoulders felt like they had been squeezed with a giant vise. He vowed he would have more empathy for his horse in the future.

The river crossing had been uneventful. Jeb had tossed a rope across the river and they had anchored it to sturdy trees on both sides. She-Bear had crossed first, wading through the current and grasping the rope as she followed it hand over hand to the opposite side. Jeb seemed to be watching her with more than casual interest and had stepped into the water unnecessarily, Ethan thought, to pull her up to the bank. With Ethan's help, and the rope as a stabilizer, Skye had struggled across the river, clutching the rope with her single hand while he anchored her narrow waist with his arm and held on to the rope with his free hand. It had been a clumsy journey, but they were greeted at the end by an excited Running Fox who raced to Skye, hugged her warmly, and then shifted to Ethan and threw his arms about his waist.

Jeb had shot a deer during Ethan's absence and they all ate heartily of venison strips Jeb roasted over the fire with She-Bear's help. The feisty Sioux woman also brewed up a concoction of deer fat and some chopped roots she had gathered from the surrounding woods with which she greased Skye's wounds and then applied to Badger Claw's scalp as well. Badger Claw had sat sullenly at the fire and eaten his share of the venison. He responded to questions asked by Skye and She-Bear in Sioux, but his responses seemed abrupt and brief. Ethan noted that Running Fox was listening attentively to the conversations among his tribesmen, and, a bit guiltily, he figured the boy would pass on any information Ethan should know.

The sun was starting to disappear over the mountain peaks, and he realized it was time for some decisions. They could not camp here indefinitely. He had hoped One Ball McLarty would have returned by now, but they should head out tomorrow morning regardless. They would follow the Powder River Trail, and, hopefully, the mountain man would intercept them before they found trouble. But he needed to talk to Skye. She seemed to be avoiding him ever since their return to the camp. And, perhaps not. He had learned quickly after their first meeting that predictability was not a Skye dePaul trait.

He heard someone moving in behind him, and he tossed a look over his shoulder. It was Skye, grasping a crudely-chopped walking stick for balance, walking unsteadily toward him. She sat down on the log that he was reclining against, her back toward him, which he thought strange.

"Thank you," she said, "for carrying me all those miles. For coming for us. I am sorry I attacked you with the knife."

"I didn't give you a choice about my carrying you, and I made the choice to try and find you. You can't be faulted for coming at me. You had no way of knowing it was me. I'm sorry I hit you. Your eye's a mess."

"My whole face is a mess."

"Your face is beautiful."

"Don't say that," she snapped.

"You know how I feel about you. I've been sick with worry. At first, I thought you were dead. That idea was unbearable."

"Jeb and Running Fox told us what you did for our village. I am grateful for that, also. Now we must free Antelope and Prairie Flower. And we must kill those bastards, every one of them." She spoke softly and without emotion.

"We will leave tomorrow morning. We will find the young women." He was not certain they would be alive.

"I became a Quaker, you know, when I was teaching at the school. I was even baptized. But I have killed, and I will kill more. I am no longer a Quaker. I have returned to the religions of my people."

"Follow the trail that gives you comfort."

"No platitudes, please. They annoy me. You cannot understand the guilt I feel. My mother and so many of my people died because of me."

"That's ridiculous. These men did not have to kill and do the terrible things they did to all the others to take you. They chose to do that."

"It has to do with gold. You said you know something about gold."

He told her about the letter from her Cheyenne lawyer, and then he plucked her father's note from his coat pocket and handed it to her. She looked at the note and passed it back.

"That is consistent with what Captain Quint told me. He knows of this gold. As a matter of fact, he stole it from an escorted military wagon. I will tell you more later. My father acquired this gold from the Cheyenne. He did not steal it . . . at least not in the sense that he was involved in the attack on military escort. But he came to possess it. Quint thought I knew where to find it."

"And you don't?"

"I did not until now. We must find the old trading post, and then after we kill these barbarians, I will show you where I think the gold may be."

"Can you travel tomorrow?"

"Yes. I am much better. I can certainly ride a horse. I have practiced many hours since I lost my hand."

"I brought Razorback with me, if you think you can handle him."

"That is good. He is a fine animal and very gentle."

"Only for you. He will be glad to see you."

She got up and walked slowly away.

22

THERE WAS AN uncomfortable chill in the air as the little caravan picked its way along a narrowing trail into the high country. Badger Claw, with a string of four ponies salvaged from his dead comrades, brought up the rear, and Skye, mounted on Razorback, rode in front of the Sioux warrior. Skye felt at home on the sorrel stallion she had ridden when she and Ethan journeyed to Lame Buffalo's village some months earlier. Ethan and everyone else who dealt with the big horse found him mean and untrustworthy, and he was kept at the Lazy R primarily for stud service for the small quarter horse herd Ethan was developing separately from his favored Appaloosas. She had argued with Ethan on more than one occasion about the relative merits of the breeds. She favored the shorter, thickly-muscled quarter horses that she considered far more practical as fast, rugged cow ponies. She told him he was just enamored with the exotic color patterns of the generally black and white Appaloosas. Perhaps one day she would challenge Ethan and Patch to a race with her and Razorback.

She gathered that Razorback was a one-person horse, for he betrayed none of his alleged unpleasantness when she rode him, and he responded unbelievably to her neck-reining, which helped greatly with her single-handed grip on the reins. She would have to see if she could buy the horse from Ethan. It would not be feasible, anyway, for him to retain Razorback for more than another generation of colts without encountering inbreeding problems in the herd.

Running Fox rode in front of her. She remembered him as an exceptionally intelligent boy, and it saddened her greatly that he had been left an orphan. His attachment to Ethan was obvious. She noticed when she got up before sunrise that the boy was burrowed in his robe only a few feet from Ethan's bedroll. Ethan pretended to tolerate the boy, but she sensed a bond, and wondered what this portended when the inevitable time to separate came.

Jeb Oaks and his pack horse trailed Ethan with She-Bear not far behind. A smile crossed her lips. The feisty She-Bear and the towering, muscular black man had formed a team from the instant of their meeting. Jeb was obviously taken with the tall, lithe She-Bear, and the woman—girl actually—did nothing to discourage him. After her experiences with the raiders, Skye would have thought She-Bear would be wary of men, but she seemed unaffected. Skye and She-Bear, with some extra blankets taken from the pack horses, had shared their buffalo robe last night, but she suspected the girl might be sharing someone else's bedroll before the journey ended. Well, that was not her concern.

Ethan raised a hand and reined Patch to a halt. He said something to Jeb, before pressing his gelding past the other riders toward Skye. As he approached, it surprised her that she had not particularly noticed before how easily he sat in the saddle and maneuvered his horse. He was an incredibly handsome man in a roguish sort of way. The black roots of a beard were forming on a face that had not been touched by a razor since departing Lockwood, she assumed, and it somehow made his steel-gray eyes seem more wolfish. Or were they coyote eyes? She could never quite shake off Lame Buffalo's vision. Did she and this man share a destiny together? He thought he loved her once, and he had nearly asked her to marry him before she cut him short. What could he see now in a one-armed half-breed with a marred and swollen face? No, she felt the moment between them had passed.

Ethan reined Patch in beside her. "How are you holding up? Are you good for two more hours?"

"I am fine. I can ride as far as we need."

"Do you recognize any of this country?"

"It has been nearly ten years since I was at the trading post. I was a young girl. This mountain country all looked alike to me. All I remember is that we came up on this side of the river . . . probably this same trail . . . and then we crossed the river before going to the trading post. It wasn't far . . . probably little more than an hour . . . but I cannot be sure."

"Well, the sun is moving toward the downside in the west. After another hour, we'll start looking for a decent campsite. I hope we hear from McLarty soon. I worry that the renegades ambushed him, but the old devil's kept his scalp a lot of years, and I find it hard to believe."

Ethan returned to the head of the column and they moved out in silence. Even Running Fox had stopped his chatter, sensing, perhaps, that danger lay ahead. An hour later, when Ethan had said they would start looking for a campsite, Skye caught sight of the ominous black harbingers of death circling the otherwise clear, blue sky some distance up the trail. No one spoke a word, but she could see the others casting uneasy glances skyward. Of course, it could be a sign of any carrion, any of a hundred rotting animal corpses inviting the scavengers to do their job in nature's scheme. She could not help, though, but think about Ethan's concern for the man called One Ball McLarty.

A half hour later, Ethan disappeared around a bend in the trail. Then the column stopped, and she saw Jeb signal She-Bear to wait, while he rode ahead to join Ethan. Soon he returned, and Skye edged Razorback ahead, so she could hear Jeb speak.

"It's one of your girls," he said. "You may want to wait a spell."

She-Bear ignored him and kneed her gelding forward, passing Jeb as she followed the course of the bend. Skye guided Razorback past Running Fox and moved quickly behind Jeb, who had wheeled and followed She-Bear. Abruptly, she stopped when she saw Ethan and She-Bear just starting to slice the leather thongs that lashed the naked Prairie Flower's hands and ankles behind her back around a sturdy pine and the wider strip that anchored her neck, as well. Her breasts were two small caverns that had obviously become buzzard delicacies following their amputation. Her body was a mass of slashes, which she instantly recognized as mates to those on her own cheek and shoulder. Someone had attacked with an insatiable rage, and she speculated she was being sent a message in case she had survived and followed. Had her own escape triggered this unspeakable brutality? She wanted to cry and scream at the injustice of all that had happened, but she was truly beyond tears, and, once again, she made a place within her to bury the outrage.

She could only watch as Ethan and She-Bear lowered the girl to the ground. Jeb had already started digging a hollow in rocky ground in the forest off the trail, chopping out tree roots that blocked the way. He would not be able to clean out more than a foot, but they would wrap her in a blanket and cover it as best they could and then stack good-sized stones over the grave and leave further mutilation to the worms and bugs that would blend her with the soil. At the end, it did not matter whether the buzzards or scavengers below the ground disposed of her, she thought. A young, innocent life was gone. Skye hoped that there was indeed something men called a soul or spirit and that Prairie Flower was in a "better place," as her Quaker friends often called it. Today, she had doubts.

Skye dismounted and helped as best as she could with the covering of the gravesite, leaving the gathering of larger stones to the men. It was a work detail made up of grim and determined faces.

While they were finishing the task, Jeb asked Ethan, "How long ago do you think since they were here?"

"It's been cool. From the condition of the body, I'd say two days . . . no more."

"Do you think they know we're following?"

"Us in particular? No. But they must suspect there could be others trailing them. This was a taunt."

Skye interrupted. "Prairie Flower was gentle and kind. But she was not strong. She would have done anything to please these animals. She was afraid to go with us for the escape. She feared we would be caught and tortured. But this is how it will end for any woman who rides with them. Antelope will last longer because she tries to satisfy the men who mount her. She even seduces them, but if we do not find her soon, she will die a terrible death, just like Prairie Flower."

Ethan said, "We will find her soon enough. It doesn't take any skill to track this many men. The question is what we do when we locate them. They far outnumber us, and we're not likely going to surprise them. We're not an army where casualties are a part of the calculation of battle. No life is expendable as far as I'm concerned. This will take all of the skill we can muster."

23

TWO DAYS LATER, Ethan reined Patch around yet another turn in the trail that followed the Powder River's increasingly twisting course as it snaked its way over the rocks and down the mountainside. He suddenly found his path blocked by the scarecrow-like figure of One Ball McLarty.

"Well, Mr. Law Wrangler, it's about time you showed up. Thought maybe your good sense might have come around and you'd headed back home."

"I was wondering about you. I hope you've been earning the money I paid out."

"I always earn my keep. If you'll just follow me about a quarter mile up the trail, I've got a camp set up back in the woods a ways that should do us fine until you make up your mind about what you want to do from here on."

McLarty turned and began walking up the trail. Ethan signaled the others to follow. Soon the mountain man turned off the river trail and angled through the trees. Ethan dismounted and led the gelding through the maze of pine until they broke into a natural clearing that would make a prime campsite with minimal axe work. As the travelers began to enter the site, McLarty stared at the entourage in apparent disbelief. Ethan, seeing the man's confusion, quickly explained. "I've recruited some help since we last talked."

"Help? Two squaws . . . and one of those looks to have caught her paw in a bear trap and mashed up her face biting it off. And then you bring another Injun that about lost his scalp, so it seems. Why, that's some army when you add them to a papoose, a darky, and a lawyer. By God, we ought to be able to whip a company of U.S. Cavalry."

Ethan resisted the temptation to respond. He was too damned tired to play the chivalrous knight defending the delicate ladies from insult. Skye would probably resent it anyway. The women in their pack seemed to defend themselves well enough. "Where can we graze the horses?" he asked instead.

"They'll have to smell it out, but there's still some decent patches of grass back in the trees to the east. I caught me a nice batch of trout if Mr. Oaks wants to see if he can make them edible. Even got half of them gutted."

Jeb and She-Bear went to work building a small cooking fire, while Running Fox and Skye gathered wood. Ethan and Badger Claw tended to the horses. Ethan was starting to get accustomed to the warrior's seemingly hostile attitude, and they communicated well enough with signs and a few words of both English and Sioux which each had come to realize the other understood. Ethan reminded himself that the warrior had lost his wife in the massacre and had undergone the embarrassment and tragedy of leading his war party into the jaws of a bloody ambush. The experience would not lighten a man's mood. He needed to cut the guy some slack. He also had to admit that he might be a bit wary because of the way the warrior constantly had his eyes on Skye. It didn't help that Running Fox had planted a seed of suspicion with his comment that Badger Claw was stalking Skye as a potential wife.

When he returned to the camp after staking out the horses, he saw McLarty standing off to the edge of the clearing with a tin plate full of roasted fish with beans and a few biscuits. The man tossed his head, signaling that Ethan should join him. Ethan would have preferred to grab his own plate of food, but he knew Jeb would hold some back.

He walked over to McLarty. The man took a bite from a biscuit and closed his eyes as he seemed to be savoring the taste. "Your darky's damned good with the pots and pans. I'll give him credit for that."

"He's not my darky, and I'd take it kindly if you would refrain from calling him that."

McLarty shrugged, "What are we going to do about those folks you're after?"

"You're the one that's been scouting them. How close are we?"

"Only a few miles. We can cross the Powder with our horses no more than a quarter mile upriver. They're holed up at an old trading post less than two miles due west of the crossing."

"They'd have their own scouts watching their backside. They'd know we're here."

"They had two scouts, as a matter of fact. I sent them on a trip down the Powder. Surprised you didn't see them along the way."

"You killed them?"

"Let's say they went to sleep last night and never woke up. Their horses are grazing with my own. Added a Sharps and a Winchester to our gun collection. Saved their coats and bedrolls, so our little army can pick over what's needed. We got three days before it snows, and we'd better be collecting gear for the storm."

"You know this for sure?"

"I do."

Ethan wasn't about to question a man who had spent a lifetime in these mountains. He had worried about storms moving in. That could be a greater threat than the raiders' guns.

"We need to make our move soon. We're outgunned by a lot."

"I'd say they're down to a dozen men."

"I'd like to cross the river tomorrow. You and I can scout out the place during the day and make our plans for an attack. I'd like to wait till right after sundown tomorrow."

"I like night. We can even the odds before a shot's fired."

"We'll talk in the morning." Ethan started to walk away.

"Law Wrangler?"

Ethan stopped and turned around. "What is it?"

"You got a claim on that one-handed squaw?"

"Her name's Skye dePaul. I don't think any man has a claim on her."

"She's some woman even with that beat-up face and half an arm. That baggy garb she's got on don't hide the female underneath. Damned if I wouldn't like to poke around in her bush awhile."

"If you try it, don't ever close your eyes again, or they'll be calling you No Balls. I guarantee it."

McLarty gave a rare grin and returned to his meal.

After supper, Ethan, Skye, and Running Fox handled the clean-up, and Ethan noticed that Jeb and She-Bear took advantage of the break to wander off in the woods. Later, they split up sentry duty, Ethan deciding that with McLarty back in camp, a single guard was sufficient. Jeb volunteered for first watch, mentioning casually that She-Bear had offered to stand watch with him. Ethan chided the cowhand a bit, reminding him not to be distracted from his duties.

While they were laying out their bedrolls for the night, Ethan saw that She-Bear was gathering up her few belongings and moving them to Jeb's bedroll. It was obvious she was changing accommodations. He was not surprised. The pair had been virtually inseparable since the young woman's arrival. It appeared Skye had ended up with the buffalo robe the two women had been sharing. Ethan looked down at Running Fox, who was just getting ready to burrow into his own robe.

"Fox," he said, "I think we're going to move." He nodded toward Skye at the opposite side of the clearing.

The boy's eyes widened, and he gave a big smile. "That good. Me think she like that but not say so. Me like it good. You like it. We all like it."

He knew that the boy would not object, but he was surprised with the enthusiasm. They started gathering up their gear and bedrolls and carrying them across the campsite. He dropped his bedroll a few feet from Skye's robe, and Running Fox laid out his robe next to Ethan's spot.

Skye was on her knees making up her own bed and looked up. "What are you doing?" she asked.

"It looks like She-Bear moved out, so we thought we'd move our stuff over here."

"You mean you think just because she leaves, you can move in."

"It's not a room or even a cabin. We just thought you wouldn't mind somebody else in the vicinity."

"Somehow I don't think this was Running Fox's idea."

The boy saved the day. "Oh, me want to be close to Sky-in-the Morning. She my friend, too. Now me be with both my friends."

Let her tell the orphan that she didn't want him near, Ethan thought. This was a hell of a smart kid. He tussled the boy's hair and winked and got an exaggerated wink back. Skye stood up and looked at them both with narrowed eyes. He thought she was fighting back a smile on tight lips.

"I guess you can sleep wherever you want. Up to a point," she quickly added.

24

THEY REGROUPED AFTER everyone had crossed the Powder River with little difficulty. They had brought the pack horses and Badger Claw's spare mounts and the extra horses McLarty had appropriated as well. Skye and She-Bear had laid claim to the dead men's coats and were cocooned in the bulk of leather and sheepskin lining. It had turned colder, and a wind had come up during the night and both had welcomed the extra cover this morning. It occurred to Ethan that the women were completely attired in garments of men recently deceased, down to the scalp that She-Bear still carried on her belt.

"We'll need to leave any horses we're not riding here," Ethan said. "Unpack and unsaddle the animals and make a stack of supplies and gear in the woods. We'll have to turn the horses loose and round them up later. They'll stay together and shouldn't stray far. There's still decent grass here and water nearby. We can't tie them or stake them out, because we don't know when we'll be back." Or if, he added silently.

When the supplies had been stashed and the extra horses released, Ethan gathered the party again. "One Ball has scouted the place where the renegades have set up camp. They've taken over an old trading post that was operated by Skye's father some years back. Skye visited here when she was a child."

"This seems like a might strange coincidence to me," McLarty piped in. "You hadn't said anything about this woman having a connection to the place."

Ethan glanced at Skye, who nodded her head somberly, which he took as her consent to tell the story. He gave a condensed version that explained that Skye's father had come into a substantial amount of gold coins and that Quint knew about it and had hoped Skye knew where they were hidden, expecting her to disclose the location.

McLarty's eyes shot sparks. "I thought we was on the trail to rescue some Indian maidens, two which done rescued themselves. Only one left at most. Is this really a goddamned treasure hunt? Are we looking to get kilt for somebody else's gold?"

"This was never a treasure hunt. Skye didn't learn about any gold until the day she escaped. We still want to free Antelope, and these men should pay for their crimes."

"I'm still in. But mark my word, if any gold gets turned up I'm expecting a fair share for my work. This raggedy-ass outfit would have been feeding buzzards way back on the trail if I wasn't around to nursemaid you."

Ethan thought the man was overstating his value to the mission, and McLarty's anger was not a welcome turn, but he decided to deal with that later. "We should be able to ride within about a half mile of the old trading post without being seen. We'll tie our horses and wait till dark before we walk in. Running Fox will stay with the horses to keep them from getting spooked. We should be to the southeast of the building site. I want Jeb and She-Bear to circle and move in from behind the cabin, and Skye and I will come from the south. One Ball and Badger Claw will take the east side. There are probably some guards posted. There's an old privy to the east of the cabin, and I'm hoping a few will make visits there. We want to kill as many as we can without firing a shot. Don't use a gun unless you have to. We'll offer their lives for Antelope's if it comes to that. Unfortunately, we're going to have to play this by ear. Any questions?"

"Yeah." It was McLarty again. "I ain't going in there with the fool Injun. Don't like him. Don't trust him. You go with him. I'll go with your woman."

"First, Skye's not my woman. But if she has no objection, I'm fine with Badger Claw." He looked over at Skye. Her dark eyes were calculating something. He could see that. And he could see both eyes now. The flesh about her eye was a kaleidoscope of purples and blacks and blues, but the swelling had subsided dramatically, and the puffiness of her damaged cheek was dissipating, although the wounds were still raw. She-Bear's concoction was doing its work, he concluded.

Skye meaningfully stroked the butt of the Army Colt that was holstered and belted around the waist of her heavy coat. "He can come with me. But remember, old man, I'm an Injun, too."

McLarty grinned rakishly. "No offense intended, Miss Skye, I got me a Cheyenne squaw I wouldn't trade for ten horses. We're going to have a little sprout any day. Already could've, for all I know, while I've been on this fool's chase."

Ethan did not like the idea of Skye pairing off with the old mountain man, but he conceded that McLarty was probably the most competent of them all when it came to killing. She was probably safer with One Ball than with himself.

25

S KYE AND MCLARTY weaved through the woods
that surrounded the old trading post. The sweet
smell of smoke from the dilapidated structure's
fireplace drifted their way and carried memories of fall
evenings she spent there with her father one trading
season. It was a calm evening, still and windless, but an
unpleasant chill was descending on the mountains. She
saw no evidence of human movement about the buildings. They had anticipated a string of guards along the
outer edges of the post and sagging stables site. This
troubled her some.

She started when she felt pressure on her rear-end
and then the harsher movement of fingers grasping her
crotch. She pulled away and wheeled around, drawing
her Colt in the same instant. McLarty loomed above her,
grinning wolfishly.

"Just checking, Missy," he said. "Nothing going on out there. I thought we could take some time to get acquainted better."

She raised the pistol, pointing it at his face. "Touch me one more time, you bastard, and I'll fire the first shot tonight," she said, her voice a near whisper.

He lifted his hands placatingly. "Just joshing. Meant no harm." His eyes focused behind her. "Something going on over there."

She turned away from him. "Where?"

"Near that old stable."

"I don't see anything," she said, just before his sinewy arm closed around her neck and began to squeeze. "Stop," she gasped. "What are you doing?"

She swung her elbow frantically against his ribs and tried to stomp on his feet and pull away, but she was caught in his vise-like grip. He just chuckled softly in response. She started to scream, but her voice choked off with more pressure clamped against her throat. Then she felt him working something over her head and face and around her neck—a rawhide loop, she decided, as she felt it tighten around her neck and draw taut before it squeezed into her flesh and panic swept over her. She dropped her gun and reached for her throat, instinctively trying to loosen the cord's suffocating grip, as her knees buckled and blackness overtook her.

When she came around, she found herself flat on her back. The pressure on her neck had eased, but the loop was still coiled around her neck. There was an abrupt tug that bit her raw flesh again, and she turned her head to see McLarty sitting on the ground less than five feet away, his hand grasping the end of the skinny, braided line that ended at her neck. She was anchored like an animal on a leash, she realized. She could not comprehend what was happening. The man's behavior made absolutely no sense.

"Glad to see you woke up, Missy. Now you listen good. We're just gonna sit here a spell. Ain't in no hurry. You and me is going to have ourselves some fun later. But we got to find your pappy's gold first. And then me and your friend, Captain Quint, got to come to some understanding about you."

"Quint?" she croaked.

"Yep. Him and me made ourselves a bargain. Now shut up."

26

ETHAN AND BADGER Claw waited behind a cluster of boulders at the forest's edge, surveying the building site. The post was well lit, and they could hear the murmur of voices from inside the structure. The quiet outside was perplexing, however. They both turned suddenly when they heard movement in the brush behind them. Ethan drew his Colt in readiness just before Running Fox appeared like a specter from the brush.

"Fox. What are you doing here?" he whispered.

"Trouble, Puma," the boy replied softly. "Bad mans, behind us. See riders near horses. I hide. Then run like antelope find you. Mans come slow. Walking now."

A trap. He couldn't believe it. McLarty had scouted the area. "How many riders, Fox?"

The boy held up one hand and one finger on the other. "This many."

"See if you can find the others and warn them. Jeb and She-Bear are there." He pointed north behind the building site. "And Skye and One Ball are there," he said, pointing to the south. "Go to Jeb first. They're closer. And before you go, tell Badger Claw."

For several minutes, Running Fox and Badger Claw were engaged in animated dialogue, and then suddenly the boy vanished into the shadowy forest.

Ethan signaled to Badger Claw to follow, and the two moved into the woods in the direction of their horses. They had not gone more than fifty paces when Ethan saw movement ahead, a creeping figure with a rifle poised for firing. He looked at Badger Claw, who held up his knife and signed that he would circle the man and approach him from the rear. Ethan nodded and inched his way in the opposite direction. As the figure stepped cautiously nearer, Ethan caught a glimpse of the Sioux warrior sneaking in behind. To distract the man, he rustled some brush and moved from behind the tree that shielded him and quickly to another. The man raised his rifle to fire, and, in the same instant, Badger Claw's knife blade slid across the stalker's throat. One down.

Shortly, they ferreted out another, but this time Ethan's blade did the work. After that, they wove quietly through the forest, darting from tree to tree as they sought another quarry. Ethan felt frustrated as time passed without any more sign of the raiders. Then a gun blast echoed in the still night, and he spun at the sound of the crunch of brush behind him. It was another of the renegades falling to the ground, his rifle clattering against loose rock. Momentarily, Jeb and She-Bear appeared in an opening in the woods some distance behind the gunman.

"He had a bead on you, Boss," Jeb said softly as he approached with a sheepish grin on his face. "But She-Bear had your back. She wanted to try my Sharps. Couldn't have done better myself."

Ethan saw that She-Bear had lagged and was now crouched over her target. "What's she doing?"

"Taking his scalp. She says this is her second scalp . . . third kill."

"Doesn't that bother you a little?"

"Boss, that woman bothers me all the time. And I hope she bothers me the rest of my life."

Ethan shrugged. There wasn't time to worry about civilizing She-Bear right now. "That gunshot's going to draw some attention this way. I suggest we spread out and see who shows up to the party."

As he predicted, it was not fifteen minutes before the others came in to view, all three of them, dispersed and walking at a snail's pace. Finally, one called out, "Jess, Diego?" He called to his comrades. "Shit, I know they came this way. There was only one shot."

Another man, with a deep southern drawl, replied. "I ain't likin' this, Hammer. Somethin' ain't right. I think we'd better back the hell out of here."

"Maybe you're right."

Ethan raised his Winchester and aimed at the man called Hammer. He squeezed the trigger, and the rifle cracked, shattering bark on a pine a few inches from the man's head. Hammer jumped behind the tree. A few minutes later he and his partners returned fire, all in Ethan's direction. He was lodged behind his own tree and wasn't about to move into the open to fire another shot, but the attackers were exposing their positions. He heard the distinctive roar of the Sharps again, followed by a grunt and a scream. "Oh shit, I'm gut shot. Hammer, help me." That would be the fourth man. And the shooter would have been Jeb. He had reclaimed his Sharps and returned She-Bear's Winchester to her, after her "try out" with the heavier weapon.

Ethan inched from behind his hiding spot and took a wild shot, and two men returned quick shots before they took off running. For some moments, a chorus of gunfire followed them, and then it was suddenly still.

Then She-Bear burst from her hiding place and raced in the direction of the renegades' retreat. "Hammer is my kill," she declared.

Jeb came up to Ethan, followed by Badger Claw. "Sorry, Boss. I think she'll outgrow this scalping business in time. It's something about these men that held her captive. She seems fine otherwise. But when it comes to these people, she turns into . . . well . . . some kind of savage."

"Puma."

Ethan turned. It was Running Fox, looking up at him with those big dark eyes, about to brim over with tears. He sensed immediately that something was terribly amiss. "What is it, Fox?"

"Sky-in-the-Morning. She taken by One Ball."

"Taken? What do you mean?"

"Like you say, me go to find and tell about bad mans. But One Ball hold her like horse with rope around neck. Me hide and watch. When guns shoot, him pull her away. Take to house. She fight hard, but him pull with rope, like pony. Me think him with bad mans."

Badger Claw looked bewildered, but obviously was aware something was wrong. Ethan said, "Fox, tell this to Badger Claw."

Ethan turned back to Jeb and She-Bear, who had just returned from retrieving a new scalp. He noticed this recent trophy was a tufted gray one. The other new blood-dripping scalp hanging from her belt was stringy blond. "You heard what Fox said?"

"Yep. Explains the trap. McLarty set it. He didn't kill any sentries out by the Powder. Damn, he even made a show of it with the horses and gear. That old man's clever as hell."

"And now we know why he made a big fuss about pairing up with Badger Claw. Somehow, he contacted Quint and made a deal to find Skye and turn her over. And I did his work for him. Hell, he was probably spying on us, too, and knew we'd found the women. Now that I think about it, he dropped his little demand over the gold share damned fast. That's because he already knew about it. I was a prize fool. I just didn't see this coming. I never suspected. But this explains why we didn't see the old man for so long."

"I didn't see it, either. I never liked the old bastard, but I didn't see him throwing in with this scum. What do we do now, Boss?"

"We get her out of there. And we give no quarter."

27

SKYE STUMBLED AND fell to her knees when she was yanked harshly into the abandoned trading post. McLarty drug her across the floor while she clutched the cord to keep from suffocating. He gave her slack at the feet of Captain Quint, who sat in a rickety straight-back chair near the fireplace. She looked up and saw the mutilated face of the barbarian leader. Most of the left side of his face was scabbed and raw. A bloody cavern had replaced his left eye, and the flesh around it was swollen and engorged with pus that intermingled with the blood and dripped down the side of his face. He glared at her contemptuously with his surviving eye, which seemed glazed over.

She refused to look up at him from the floor and clumsily got to her feet. She stood there, no more than five feet from him, and met his stare. She was certain death would visit her before she left this place, and she shuddered at the thought of what kind of death that might be. She could only hope that it came quickly.

"Welcome home, bitch," Quint said, his voice raspy. "Do you remember this place?"

It was then that she noticed his pallid skin and the trembling of the hands that rested on his lap. This man's body, she guessed, raged with infection. He was probably going to die from the wound she had inflicted, but he was far from conceding it. And he would not die soon enough to save her life.

"Answer me, bitch. I asked you a question."

"Yes, I remember."

"Did you hear the gunfire outside?"

"Yes."

"That was the execution of your friends. We will let you live long enough to see their stinking corpses. You may thank Mr. McLarty for that. It was his idea we set this little trap, and he sprung it pretty good it looks like."

She looked at McLarty, who still held the cord and stood next to Quint, leering tauntingly at her. "We'll find out soon enough if his trap worked or not, won't we?"

She saw a flash of doubt cross McLarty's eyes, and he tossed a glance at the door. Her remark also struck Quint, for he ordered a skinny, narrow-faced man called

Rat to go outside and see how soon the others would be bringing in the bodies. It hit her then that she might never say the things she had promised herself she would say someday to Ethan, the patient, good man who was always on her side, always at her side—when she would allow him. God, please let him be alive. She knew now. The doubt had vanished.

"Take that goddamned axe away from the bitch. How did she get in here with that thing?"

Quint's words confused her for a moment. Then she remembered the little hatchet still hung in her belt. She had dropped the Colt in the woods, but she still had her remaining weapon. She reached for the hatchet instinctively with no notion of what she was going to do with it. Too late. McLarty jerked the cord sharply, sending a wave of pain through her skull, and then he stepped toward her and yanked the hatchet from the belt. He handed it to Quint, who looked at it strangely and then dropped the tool on the floor.

Quint seemed to be lost somewhere in his mind, so for the first time her eyes scanned the large room, counting eight men, including Quint and McLarty, a few sitting on the straight-back chairs and others dozing or sitting on the floor. Where was Antelope? The question was answered when the door to the single sleeping room

Skye used to occupy on her rare visits opened, and the girl came out with the big Negro the renegades called Goliath. Her face and arms were marked with scratches and bruises. She had not fared well since She-Bear and Skye escaped. Skye still worried the escape had been the cause of the brutality directed at the remaining girls. Her eyes met Antelope's, and she was relieved that she still saw hope there.

"Now, bitch, we talk about the gold." Quint had returned to the world. "At our last meeting, you promised you would tell me where to find the gold. You broke your promise. You're going to die for what you did to me, but if we find the gold, you get it quick. We'll start with this here axe. One finger at a time. You can see how it feels to lose both paws. Then we'll do your tits with a skinning knife." He spoke without emotion. He seemed strangely detached, more like he was an observer than a participant.

She wondered if he had lost his senses. Perhaps it was the infection that was destroying his mind. No matter. Her future looked bleak. He would not keep his word about a quick death. She faced torture before the end of her life. All she could do was buy time. "I do know where the gold is hidden. You will not find it in this building or anyplace nearby. I will lead you to it in the morning."

"Just tell me."

"I cannot. I have not been here since I was a little girl. I would not know how to explain. But when I see the landmarks, I will know."

"You're lying, of course, but we will wait."

McLarty interrupted. "While we're waiting for the sun to come up, I want this woman. If I can have the little room for an hour, I'll show her something she ain't never seen. She thinks she's too damn good for me."

Quint did not even look at him but replied matter-of-factly. "She is too damn good for you. She's mine first. You can have the leftovers. But you might be humping a dead woman."

"In your shape, you ain't going to be humping anything."

"Mr. McLarty, shut up and drop your ass on the floor. You're outnumbered here, and you're a dead man if I say so."

McLarty let himself down to the floor, giving a yank on Skye's leash and pulling her to the floor with him. He leaned up against the wall near the fireplace, and Skye welcomed the heat. She observed that her hatchet lay on the floor within a few paces, although the odds of her fighting her way out of the place with an axe were laughable. McLarty moved closer to her, pressing his hip against her own. He placed his hand on her thigh and began kneading it with his fingers. Her instincts were to slap it away, but that would mean a jerk on the neck cord, which had already chewed into her flesh to the point of drawing blood. She turned her face away from him to avoid the smell of him, the sour sweat and rancid breath.

Quint spoke again. "Bitch, have you seen this gold?"

"No."

"Then how do you know it's there?"

"I don't."

"But your old man told you?"

"He gave me a letter." She decided the truth would do no harm now. The time for playing games had passed.

"I want to see this letter."

"I don't have it."

"Where is it?"

"I left it with my lawyer."

"Who's your lawyer?"

"Ethan Ramsey."

McLarty chimed in. "That's the bastard who's chasing after your bunch."

"No more. The boys ought to be dragging his corpse in anytime now." He turned his eye toward the door. "Where's Rat?"

28

THEY HAD RETURNED to the little rock fortress east of the trading post that Ethan and Badger Claw had positioned themselves in earlier. The location afforded a good view of the front cabin door, which was apparently the only usable opening. Jeb had sneaked up to the rear of the building earlier and tested the back door finding it set fast and concluding it had been nailed shut, probably when the structure was abandoned.

They watched as the front door opened, and a short, wiry man stepped out. He stood for some moments a few feet from the doorway, evidently making a survey of the landscape before he closed the door behind him. He rolled and lighted a cigarette before moving out into the clearing. Obviously nervous and wary, he didn't walk more than fifty feet away from the house. He was no doubt expecting the other renegades to show up, perhaps with a horse train of bodies, to report their mission had been accomplished. He would be eager to return to the cabin.

Ethan tapped Badger Claw on the shoulder to get his attention, and then signed that he should retrieve his bow and nock an arrow. Pointing to the thin man, Ethan's instructions were clear. The warrior gave a rare smile and then, with his bow and a quiver of arrows, slipped away into the woods. No more than ten minutes later, an arrow lodged in the wiry man's throat, and, before he sunk to the ground, a second drove into his chest.

Running Fox said, "Him good warrior, yes?"

Ethan grudgingly agreed. "Yes, he's a very good warrior." For that matter he had come to like and respect the man. Badger Claw had earned his respect the last several days, and Ethan had come to trust and rely on him.

"Another down. But there's a house full inside, and when somebody finds this man, they'll be on the alert. We can't go charging in there. They have us outgunned, and it would put Skye and Antelope in even more danger. And we can't leave Skye with those men all night. God knows what they'll do to her . . . especially with the damage she must have done to this Quint. We may be too late as it is." Even as he spoke, he refused to believe his own words.

Jeb said, "Boss, we could smoke them out."

"Block the chimney?"

"Yep. We did that a good many times when I rode with the U.S. Cavalry, and we were taking down Comancheros and other renegades at their hideouts. Got a nest of Kiowa that squatted in a settlor's house once."

"That would bring them out. But would they kill the women first?"

"More likely to make shields of them. But I don't see how we get this done without some risks."

"No, you're right, of course. It's the best idea that's showed up so far. Let's do this. You and She-Bear position yourselves with the rifles, maybe one to the east and one to the south. Can you see well enough in the dark to hit somebody from this distance?"

"We've got some moonlight. We can hit somebody. Challenge will be not to shoot Skye or Antelope. But we'll just be damn sure when we squeeze the triggers. We'll have to wait till they spread out some."

"And don't shoot Badger Claw and me."

"Why would we do that?"

"Because we'll be waiting right outside the door. We'll try to separate Skye and Antelope from the others or kill anybody who thinks he's going to use one of them for a shield. Before we do that, we'll stuff the chimney. If we take the coats from the dead men we left out in the woods, that should work fine."

"I don't know about this hand to hand idea, Boss."

"Jeb, I won't be sitting up here safe and snug when Skye comes out that door. Besides, you know I'm just as likely to shoot one of our own trying to hit somebody with a rifle from this range."

Jeb grinned. "I can't argue that. Okay, me and She-Bear will get set up."

29

NOBODY LEAPED UP to go look for Rat when Captain Quint ordered it, so Goliath went out to check. Skye noticed the men didn't seem so fearful of Quint now, and given his obvious physical deterioration, that was understandable. The man was walking death, and she had been the cause of it. That was a sobering thought, and she unsuccessfully chided herself for not feeling some remorse. She guessed she was becoming a callous and wicked woman.

They all knew about the gold now, and they were hanging around for their cut. She assumed that Quint had not planned on a split. McLarty had probably been promised a share and, perhaps, Goliath, who seemed to be Quint's second-in-command, but she was confident the others were in for a pittance, and most were probably stupid enough to settle for that. Who would end up with the gold if they found it? It was hard to say, but it was certain many would die before the day for dividing the spoils arrived.

McLarty still had his hand on her thigh, but at least his fingers had tired. She cast a sideways glance and saw that his eyes were closed and that his chin was resting on his chest. She knew that was deceptive, though, because she doubted he ever truly slept when danger lurked nearby. Until tonight she had not thought she could ever despise a man more than Quint, but McLarty had pulled ahead in that race. Quint was an evil, vicious man, who did not pretend to be otherwise. McLarty, though, was a traitor whose colors changed like a chameleon's when opportunity presented. He was the more dangerous man.

Most of the men were nodding off or dozing when Goliath burst through the door and slammed it shut. "Captain Quint," he yelled, startling Quint so much he almost tumbled from his chair.

"Goddammit, Goliath, what is it? You almost scared the shit out of me." Strangely, Quint did not raise his voice, sounding like he was reading a script when he spoke.

"I found Rat. He's out front with two arrows sticking in him."

That captured everyone's attention, and the men began to get up and reach for their weapons. Goliath marched over to Quint and looked down at his employer, who was still fastened to his chair with a confused look in his single eye. Skye felt a sharp tug on her neck as McLarty stood up, so she got off the floor, too. As she did, she thought the smoke from the fireplace was starting to irritate her eyes.

"What do we do, Captain?"

"About what?"

"Rat."

"I don't know. What do you want to do about him?"

Skye thought Quint was acting like a drunk. It appeared Goliath was coming around to the realization that his captain was no longer in command of either his faculties or the troops.

"There's Indians out there, men. Two of you get to the window," Goliath yelled.

The only window was no more than two feet square and covered with a single gunny sack, so unless they tore the bag off, Skye didn't see how men posted at the window would help much. She suddenly found herself starting to cough, and she noticed several of the men were also.

McLarty stepped over to Quint and looked him over. He turned to Goliath and said, "This guy couldn't find that box of gold if it was in his own bed. Somebody's got to take charge here."

"I guess that would be me," the big man said, as he began to cough.

McLarty started coughing, too. "They plugged the chimney," he yelled as the smoke started rolling into the room. "Tear that sack off the window."

Someone obeyed, but the smoke was too heavy now, and McLarty dropped to the floor to suck more air into his lungs. Skye followed and, at the same time, snatched up the hatchet. Goliath grabbed Quint's arm and started to lead him to the window. Two men, coughing and choking, barged out the door. Skye heard two gunshots and knew she had been given another chance at life. She looked around the room, seeking Antelope, and saw her curled in a corner in a fetal position. She had to get to her. She turned back to McLarty. He was on his hands and knees, inching toward the door. She had no choice but to follow him, but there was slack in the cord. She focused on the hand that clutched it, waiting for those fingers to touch the floor to hold his weight. When that hand came down, she raised her arm and arced the hatchet downward with all her strength. The blade sliced through the knuckle of McLarty's left hand, and she saw at least two bloody fingers drop on the splintered floor. Most important, the cord fell loose and she pulled it back and was finally free.

McLarty roared in agony and clutched his mangled hand. She got a glimpse of the anguished and enraged face before she crawled away into the smoke. She reached Antelope and grabbed her hand. The girl saw who it was, but she was nearly overcome by the smoke and had tears streaming down her face and refused to budge. Skye refused to leave her and huddled with her in the corner, pressing the girl's head close to the floor with hers, hoping to search out air. Through the haze, she saw several other men escaping through the now open doorway, and then she heard more gunshots. Several sounded very close.

She could not locate McLarty in the melee, but she saw Goliath dragging Quint toward the open door. Then someone leaped in the doorway and evidently saw her through the smoke. He raced toward them, a war club in one hand. It was Badger Claw. She saw Goliath release Quint, who dropped to the floor. The big man pulled his pistol and aimed at Badger Claw's back. She screamed a warning, but before Goliath squeezed the trigger a gunshot cracked, and a pool of blood spread on the big man's temple as his legs crumpled, and he dropped like lead to the floor.

Suddenly, Ethan was by her side, helping her to her feet, and Badger Claw lifted Antelope into his arms and was carrying her to the door and out into the darkness. She and Ethan followed close behind. A blast of cold struck her as they stepped outside, but she welcomed the fresh air and gratefully drew it into her lungs, coughing occasionally to kick out the irritating smoke.

It took her a few moments to realize Ethan was embracing her in his arms. It was not a bad place to be right now, she thought, and she gave into it, clutching him tightly. Neither spoke a word until she said, "I thought I'd never see you again."

"I'm not that easy to escape from," he said.

"Maybe it's time for me to stop running," she said meaningfully.

30

ETHAN UNPLUGGED THE chimney flue while Jeb and Badger Claw began the macabre task of removing the scattered bodies. The frozen, rocky ground made burial of more than a dozen bodies impossible, so after salvaging coats, weapons, and any other items that might prove useful, they dumped the dead men in a nearby ravine. They could feed the buzzards and any other scavengers that happened by. Besides, Ethan figured, why should this scum have more royal treatment than the villagers they murdered?

The three women and Running Fox had left to retrieve the saddle horses, although, with the addition of the renegades' animals and gear, they were in no danger of being left afoot. At daylight, they would recover their own supplies and the pack and spare horses that had not wandered off.

As the smoke cleared from the trading post, Ethan entered the building, expecting to find more bodies. He discovered two, plus a man's severed thumb and forefinger. Captain Quint's pale, emaciated form lay crumpled on the floor not far from the corpse of Goliath. It appeared the smoke had finished him off. Dragging Quint across the splintered floor and out of the building was easy enough, but he had to recruit Jeb to help with the big man, and it required the three of them to escort Goliath to his last resting place. Then it occurred to Ethan that One Ball McLarty's body had not turned up.

He asked Jeb, "Have you or Badger Claw found McLarty's body?"

"I was thinking the same thing, Boss. I haven't seen a sign of the creepy bastard."

"I know he was in the trading post. Skye said she took her hatchet to his hand, and I found a thumb and finger on the floor."

"At least she doesn't take scalps."

"I don't know. Nothing would surprise me about the woman. Nothing. I'll feel better when we find McLarty, but we'll probably have to wait till daylight. There's a good supply of wood in the post. Let's build the fire back up and cover the window and spend the night there. I don't like the wind that's coming up."

"You'll get no quarrel from me on that idea."

The men had the fire going and the worst of the blood wiped off the floor by the time Skye and the others returned with the horses. The old trading post looked like business had reopened with the stacks of saddles, guns, coats, and blankets that had been gathered at one end of the room. Quint's renegade army had been well-supplied, and Jeb had searched out some bags of beans and flour and jerky that would shore up their own dwindling food supplies.

Ethan pulled his timepiece from his pocket. It was nearly three o'clock. It had been a busy night. He told Jeb and She-Bear to take the old sleeping room if they wanted, unless they wanted to be closer to the fireplace. Jeb, with a suggestive wink, said they'd be plenty warm, and the two collected extra blankets from the appropriated goods and disappeared.

Running Fox was already dug into his robe and sleeping off to one side of the fireplace. Ethan tossed a few more logs on the fire and laid out his bedroll next to the boy. Without invitation, Sky put her buffalo robe a few feet from Ethan. That felt right somehow. He noticed that on the other side of the fireplace, Antelope and Badger Claw, with a respectable distance between them, had seemingly started to pair off. The girl was nothing if not resilient. But it was damned hard to survive this country without that trait, he guessed. There was nearly half a ton of resilience sleeping in the old trading post tonight.

As he pulled a blanket over his shoulders, Skye, snuggled in her robe nearby, spoke softly, "Ethan?"

"Yes?"

"You didn't find McLarty, did you?"

"No. We'll look again after sunup."

"You will not find him."

"How can you be so sure?"

"I do not know if he can be killed. He seems to be protected by evil spirits. I would not be surprised if he grew new fingers."

"He's just a man. And he's a badly hurt man. If we don't find his body, he's probably off someplace dying. He's no threat to us now."

"Not now, but I fear we have not seen the last of him."

"I fear we're not going to get some sleep." He pulled the blanket over his ears.

"Ethan?"

"Will you help me find the gold in the morning?"

"Do you think we can find it?"

"I think so."

"Okay, we can try." Again, he tugged his blankets around him. He started to nod off to sleep.

"Ethan?"

What in the hell did she want now? "Yes."

"When McLarty brought me here, I thought I might never see you again. Then, I knew."

"Knew what?"

"That I did not ever want to be separated from you again."

He could not believe what he was hearing. "I do not want us to be separated either. I never did."

"Ethan, you would be warmer in my robe."

"Do you mean—"

"Yes, I do mean."

He abandoned his blankets and slipped under the buffalo robe and onto the layered confiscated blankets that cushioned the rough floor. Her body melted into his and his arms encircled her. He savored her closeness for some moments, and then his lips found hers and lingered, brushing gently before devouring. The urgency struck him even before her fingers touched him. He helped Skye remove her garments, and she helped as best she could with his. When they were naked, there was no holding back, and their coupling was frantic. Later, there was patience and gentleness, and they finally fell asleep with Ethan spooned against her back, his arm flung over her breasts.

31

WHEN ETHAN AWAKENED, daylight was sifting through the burlap sack that covered the window opening and a fire was crackling in the fireplace and tossing warmth his way. He was acutely aware of the naked body that still snuggled against his own, and, under other circumstances, he would have been more than ready to take advantage of Skye's proximity. Ethan pulled the robe back a bit and peaked out. Running Fox was up and warming himself in front of the fire, and Jeb appeared to have a Dutch oven doing its work on some hot coals off to one side of the fireplace. There would at least be some biscuits for breakfast. He had intended to return to his own bedroll before anyone else got up, but he had dropped off into a sated sleep. It appeared Skye was still lost in slumber land.

"Morning, Boss. Hope you had a good sleep," Jeb said, grinning broadly.

Ethan was glad that the cowhand could not see his blushing face. "Uh, yeah, we all needed some rest, I guess."

Running Fox interjected, "Puma, me worry when not see you in blankets. Then see where you be. Happy you not lost."

Now what in the hell did that mean? He started searching for his clothes and found his shirt twisted between Skye's feet. His britches were on the floor next to the sleeping robe. After he had located all the pieces of his sparse wardrobe, he maneuvered into the garments while managing to remain covered with the robe. Skye slept on, oblivious. Finally, he crawled out from under the robe and left her sleeping there.

He went outside to relieve his bladder, and when he returned, he saw that Badger Claw and Antelope were missing. She-Bear was helping with breakfast. "Where are our friends?" he asked.

Jeb replied, "They're going to try to find us another deer . . . or maybe an elk. Antelope will help skin and butcher it. It's getting so damned cold, we won't have to worry about keeping the meat fresh, and Badger Claw insists snow is coming in tomorrow."

"I guess it's best to stay put then. If we have the option of shelter here, it makes no sense to be out on the trail in a snow storm. McLarty had said something about snow, too. I wouldn't bet against anything the two agreed upon."

"We should get the pack horses that we left by the Powder and pick up all the gear and few foodstuffs we have left and bring them back here. I don't know what we're going to do with all the horses we're ending up with. Anyway, I thought me and She-Bear and Badger Claw . . . and maybe Antelope . . . would head out after breakfast and try to take care of that job, if that's okay with you."

"More than okay. I promised Skye I'd go on the treasure hunt with her this morning. It's probably like looking for that pot of gold at the end of a rainbow. But we need to get it done."

"Don't make fun of my gold, law wrangler. You'll see soon enough." Ethan turned toward Skye's voice and was mildly surprised to see her sitting on top of the blankets, slipping into her ragged buckskins, seemingly unconcerned that one of her small breasts was quite exposed as she pulled the shirt over her head. The room was dusky, though, so he supposed one didn't have to make many concessions to modesty.

Ron Schwab

"Glad you decided to get up."

She stood up. "You sure don't have any apologies coming, but I guess I should send them Jeb's way. I'm not doing my share this morning. It won't happen again. I don't expect breakfast served in bed. On second thought . . . "

Badger Claw and Antelope returned with two does, and Jeb helped the warrior lash together a crude pine rack in front of the post on which to hang the skinned, gutted carcasses. Afterward, the two men rode off with She-Bear and Antelope to retrieve the pack animals and gear. At Jeb's coaxing Running Fox joined the group. Ethan saw this as a healthy sign. He was finding that the Sioux boy was growing on him and becoming more than special, but the clinging, for both their sakes, needed to be ending, and it was starting to happen. And now, especially, he needed some time with Skye to sort out what had happened between them during the night. He was concerned she might be having second thoughts, although her mood was cheerful considering all that she had endured these past weeks.

Skye and Ethan rode in the opposite direction with Razorback and Patch leading two spare horses with empty saddles and extra saddle bags, Skye's idea for packing the gold coins she seemed confident she was going to find. They rode side by side, and from time to time he furtively cast glances her way. His eyes were drawn to her bruised and scabbed face, and he saw nothing but stunning beauty there. She was lost in thought, but, from the first, their comfortable silences together had been an attraction. He knew some folks who would be uneasy with such quiet moments, but he was not one for constant chatter. He treasured his thinking time and enjoyed his own company.

"Do you think I'm a slut?" Skye asked.

"What?"

"Do you think I'm a slut? For seducing you last night? I don't think my Quaker friends would approve of my behavior. I suppose I'm going to go to hell now. I've killed men and done violence to others. Even worse, the Sioux frown upon a woman giving herself to a man before the marriage. And now I've fornicated."

He had to hold back his smile. "Well, if it makes you feel better, you didn't really have to do much seducing. I wasn't a reluctant participant."

"The Sioux attitude about these things is mostly custom. The Lakota Great Spirit does not object to fornicating as near as I know. The whites always worry about sinning and feel guilty about enjoying it. Do you feel guilty?"

"Not a bit. But I'd feel more comfortable if we were married."

They rode along in silence for better than fifteen minutes. They had picked up a well-used deer trail and she seemed to be casting her eyes for landmarks. She nudged Razorback into the lead and called back to him. "I'll marry you when this is over, if you still want that."

He could not believe it. He had made kind of an offhand proposal, and she had accepted. It was hard to contain the euphoria that struck him. "I'll still want it. I've wanted to marry you for a long time. Remember, you all but turned me down once."

"You should have been more persistent. Will you still share my robe even if we aren't married yet?"

"If you wish."

"And we can still fornicate?"

"By all means."

"I forgot to mention something, though. You can change your mind if it is a problem."

"What's that?"

"I won't obey."

He didn't know what she was talking about. "I don't understand."

"I attended church weddings while I was teaching at the Quaker school and when I lived in Cheyenne. During the vows the wife promises to obey her husband. I would not do that. Well, I might be willing to promise, but I would not keep the promise. Very unlikely, I would say."

"I have no problem with that. We can negotiate differences."

"That is not fair. You are a lawyer."

"Have I won an argument with you yet?"

She didn't speak for another five minutes. "We've got a deal then?"

"We've got a deal."

The horses broke into the open at the base of a peak. "Please don't tell me we've got to climb to the top of this peak to find your pot of gold," he said.

"No. It should be in some rocks along the bottom here, to the south a short distance. I came here many times . . . twice with my father . . . to watch a badger."

"A badger. Like the badger mentioned in your father's letter."

"Yes. His spelling was not quite right, but I knew immediately what he was writing about. We found this badger den when we were riding one morning, and we saw a huge badger come out. He just ignored us and went into the woods for his daily hunt. I was totally fascinated by him and came back many times to see if I could spot him again, and I almost always did about the same time each morning. I kept my distance, and he might look my way .

. . I know he saw me . . . but he would just lumber off and go about his business."

"There's a promising badger residence." Ethan pointed to a cluster of boulders at the base of the peak. Three or four feet above was a hole barely large enough for a badger to squeeze through, but Ethan had seen the openings of a good many badger dens and was sure Skye's badger or a relative had dug this one.

"This is the one. I know it is," she yelled, as she dismounted and raced for the hole.

"Wait," Ethan said. "What if someone's home?"

She stopped and waited at the rocks while Ethan searched and came up with a dead pine limb about five feet long and approached the hole. "Be ready to run," he warned, "in case we wake somebody up." He poked the limb in the hole, stabbing repeatedly, and it took a few moments for him to realize the tip of the wood was striking metal. He tossed the stick aside and leaned down, extending his hand almost an arm's length into the den.

"You found it didn't you?" Skye said with "I told you so" in her voice.

He was certainly feeling metal, very rusted his touch indicated. He moved his hand over the rough surface, getting a sense of the shape, inching his fingers down the side of what had to be a box of some kind until he felt a handle. He grabbed and pulled, grunting, as it took all the strength he could muster to guide the box, inch by inch, to the den's opening.

32

SKYE AND ETHAN lugged the saddlebags into the trading post and piled them in a corner as far away from the door as possible. They had not counted the coins, but the metal box had been nearly full. There was not time to count now, but she didn't see that it mattered. It was a fortune in her eyes.

It was mid-afternoon, and the others had not returned yet, so at her suggestion, she and Ethan took advantage of some private time under the buffalo robe. She had been mostly joking when she asked Ethan if she was a slut, but she wondered what kind of a person she had suddenly become. She had never imagined she would be like this with a man. Ethan did not seem to mind, though. And in the throes of passion, she had actually said, "I love you." He had responded in kind. He had professed his love months back when she had cut off his proposal, but this was a first for her. Strange that she had accepted a man's offhand offer of marriage, and she had not ever told him she loved him. But she would tell him again. And again. She must never let him doubt it, even when she was angry.

She heard the hoofbeats and the voices signaling the return of their friends and went outside to greet them. Ethan was already near the run-down stable. He had been trying to upright the old corral and was cutting pine branches and dragging in timber to form a wind-break along the fence to both fortify it and offer some protection from the wind and snow.

The horse herd they had accumulated nearly filled the stable, which was just a single open room without par-titions to offer some protection from the weather, but since the doors had long since collapsed, the animals were free to roam into the small lot outside the building. They would have to lead them to the nearby stream and break the ice for the horses to drink, and she was not cer-tain how they would feed a herd this size.

While the others helped finish the fence work, Skye recruited Running Fox to help her prepare some sup-per, conceding to herself that with her missing hand she would do more good feeding their crew than repair-ing the corral. Jeb had already sliced some venison for steaks, so she had Running Fox assist with roasting the strips while she boiled some pinto beans. Earlier she had rounded up tin plates and forks formerly possessed by the renegades and cleaned them with boiling water.

From the attack on the food and the compliments that were tossed her way, she decided she and Running Fox had prepared an edible meal. As they ate, Ethan told the others, "We found the gold." He nodded toward the corner where they had stacked the saddle bags. "I guess disposing of that is between Skye and the U.S. government."

"Our immediate concern is the horses. Counting all the pack horses and Badger Claw's ponies, we've got thirty-five or more animals to feed and water. We need to get out of here as soon as possible, so they can forage as we go. We may have more critters than we can handle, anyway." He paused while She-Bear interpreted for Badger Claw and Antelope. The warrior replied at length, waving his hands excitedly.

She-Bear interpreted, "He says he must have five horses. Antelope demands these before she will be his woman. He is upset about it, because horses are not given to a wife but to the father, who is dead. A wife does not have property of her own. But Antelope is insisting. He has five horses, but if he gives those to her, he will be a pauper and cannot enter the marriage with less than she."

"Tell him he can have his pick of six of the renegades' horses for his good work here. He will then have one more horse than Antelope."

She-Bear explained to the warrior, who smiled and nodded approvingly. He then spoke again at some length before She-Bear translated. "He says you are a wise man and worthy of mating with Sky-in-the-Morning. He accepts now that she will not be his wife and believes in Lame Buffalo's vision that you and Sky-in-the-Morning share a destiny. He does have another concern, though."

"What's that?"

"He says we are being watched by Cheyenne. He has seen fresh sign, and he saw a warrior lurking in the woods when we were returning with the horses and supplies."

"There haven't been any attacks lately. Those who haven't been driven to the reservations have had the good sense to lay low. If there's no trouble, the soldiers aren't that interested in looking for them. Ask him if he thinks they will bother us."

Skye spoke now, and she and Badger Claw engaged in an extended dialogue before she turned to Ethan. "He does not think they will seek trouble now, although they might steal some horses. They are trying to keep the peace until spring when Custer and the pony soldiers will come. Then the war drums will begin. Some of the young braves in our village have already joined the Cheyenne and our Lakota brothers. He did not say this, but I have been told there was a sun dance in the summer where the tribes gathered and formed an alliance in preparation for the spring. Sitting Bull of the Hunkpapa is, perhaps, the most important leader. Most Brule leaders are not a part of this, but the chiefs cannot control all the braves and warriors."

"But this doesn't have anything to do with us."

Skye said, "I think Badger Claw is making the point that the Northern Cheyenne and Sioux are at peace now. Perhaps you have not thought about it, but you and Jeb are the only persons in this room who are not of Sioux Blood. Badger Claw would like to parley with the Cheyenne. He thinks they would trade for horses and guns. If we do not trade, they will take. We could be rid of the burden of so many horses and have some furs and other goods we do not have to feed."

"Was this Badger Claw's idea or yours?"

"He agreed with my thoughts on the subject."

"And you were a teacher? You should have been a pirate."

"So, you agree, he should parley?"

"We have nothing to lose, I guess."

"Fine. I told him he should do this. He will sleep a few hours and then leave in the night. He wishes to be back when the sun is overhead. Tomorrow night the snow comes."

"Why did you bother to ask me?"

"We are partners, are we not?"

Everyone pitched in with clean up. Then Skye and She-Bear began sorting out the guns, blankets and clothing, holding back a few of the shirts and trousers they felt they might use. Running Fox helped and seemed to enjoy taking on the tasks assigned to him by the two women. Antelope and Badger Claw had been given the extra room, so the warrior could catch some rest before departing. It seemed, with promise of the horse dowry, they were an official couple now.

Skye studied the merchandise as they lined it up along the front wall. Her Indian friends were increasingly adapting the white man's clothing to their own uses, and the coats would be especially useful. The blankets, she found, worked nicely as a buffer between the coarseness of a buffalo robe or deerskin, and there were fewer robes being produced these days with the disappearance of the buffalo. She spotted a smaller pistol she liked and held it back with its holster and gun belt. It weighed less than her Colt. She decided at that instant she was going to become a marksman. She intended to learn everything there was to know about her gun, especially how to use it. Ethan would give her lessons tomorrow—or perhaps Jeb. His military training should make him a qualified instructor. She picked out a Winchester that caught her eye, also. She had assumed that she would be unable to handle a rifle because she had lost much of her lower left arm, but she could still form a crook with her elbow, and she increasingly found herself unconsciously using what remained of her appendage to help with tasks.

Later, as they were bedding down for the night, Skye told Ethan about her plans for shooting lessons. He seemed to think it was a good idea but backed away from taking on teaching responsibilities.

"We'd get into a fuss," he said. "Besides, Jeb's a better shot than I am and knows a lot more about the workings of the guns. Talk to him in the morning."

With Ethan's help, Skye spread out the robe and blankets they would share. No sense in pretense. She sensed that Ethan was uneasy about something, though. "What is it?" she asked.

Running Fox had pulled his robe closer to the fire, separated from Skye and Ethan by a strong dozen feet, and was just crawling into his nest. Ethan spoke in a near whisper. "Do you think he is bothered by us? I mean by our sleeping together? I guess I'm not a very good example."

"Ethan, he's moved away because he sees us as a couple now. Remember, he has lived in a tipi where the entire family sleeps. Mother and father share a robe and children are sometimes just a few feet away. Some nights the father may move to the robe of another wife. The children are aware that men and women do more than sleep under the robes. But this is life as they know it, and it does not occur to them that things should be otherwise. This is not my preference. I look forward to more private times with you. That will be a new adventure," she said suggestively. "But Running Fox accepts this. I daresay, he may even be finding some comfort in our being together. Now do not tell me you want to go back to your own bedroll?"

He replied by joining her under the robe.

33

"THE SKY DOESN'T look so threatening right now," Jeb said, as he and Ethan each led a pair of horses to the edge of the woods, looking to scare up some grass where they might stake out the animals. "Maybe we should have headed out of this place."

"I would have, but we would have had to leave most of the horses behind. Trying to herd this many on the trail would have slowed us so much, it would have tripled our time moving down the mountain."

It was late morning and they had been outdoors rotating the horses to grass and water since shortly after sunrise. Skye, She-Bear, and Antelope helped most of the morning but had returned to the post to put together a meal. After leaving the horses, they had started back to the stables when Ethan suddenly sensed movement in the forest. "We'd better get to the post," he said, his voice muted and level. "We've got company."

"I don't see anything."

"Neither do I, but I know somebody's out there."

They veered away from the stables and hurried toward the trading post door, but before they reached it, Badger Claw appeared astride his horse, followed by a dozen Cheyenne warriors who emerged like silent ghosts from the trees, leading horses packed with furs and animal skins. His companions were well armed and grim-faced but not otherwise menacing. Ethan stood in front of the door and awaited the visitors' approach. He told Jeb, "Why don't you tell the women we have company, and we'll need either Skye or She-Bear to translate."

Momentarily, Skye appeared and greeted the warriors with a smile and spoke to Badger Claw in Sioux. The warrior replied at some length and then signed to the Cheyenne while he haltingly used words of their language or, perhaps, Ethan thought, some shared vocabulary.

While Badger Claw and the Cheyenne conversed, Skye explained, "The Cheyenne are camped just two miles from here. They're moving their village to the lower valleys. When spring comes, they are joining up with many Sioux and Cheyenne somewhere north to await Custer. Badger Claw plans to take Antelope and join them. But they are not at war with us. They want to trade for horses and guns."

"The horses are a burden to us, and I'm glad to trade all we don't need. The guns are another matter. I can't trade guns that are going to be used against United States soldiers."

"They can take the guns from us anyway, and there is nothing we could do but die."

"It's illegal for us to sell them guns, and it's not right with what we're being told. I don't want that on my conscience."

"I will talk trade with them. Badger Claw has already told them we have guns. Why don't you go in, and you and Jeb can hide most of the guns and leave a few rifles and some of the pistols out for trade? They will not have enough experience with sidearms to do real harm."

This made sense. Skye had an innate practicality that had a way of leading them to sensible compromise. He entered the cabin, and in a short time, he and Jeb had squirreled the best rifles and most of the ammunition under loose floorboards and in their robes and blankets, which they stacked in the corner atop the saddle bags full of gold. No sooner had they finished the task than Skye entered with Badger Claw and a half dozen Cheyenne warriors toting tightly bound furs and skins.

Ethan watched while Skye took charge of the bartering. It fascinated him to watch the enigma who had captured his heart bargain animatedly with the Cheyenne while, with Badger Claw's help, she made clear what she expected. She would shake her head from side to side many times, taking a Cheyenne warrior to the brink of anger, before granting an affirmative nod. She turned to Ethan and Jeb. "Start gathering up the horses. Separate out ours and the ones we need. The others will be sold before I am finished here. Remember we will have animal pelts and the gold to carry out when we leave, besides our gear and food supplies."

Ethan replied, "If you think you're going to end up with all the pelts, we'd better have six pack horses."

"I will have all of the pelts. Badger Claw and Antelope are to have first pick of the remaining horses, and the Cheyenne will take what's left over."

As Ethan and Jeb headed for the stables to separate their own mounts and pack horses from the herd they had accumulated, Jeb said, "I think your Skye dePaul carries on her papa's trading blood."

"Yes, from the day I met her, she's always got the best of me." He smiled and shook his head in disbelief. "But I think if she's going to keep me, I'm getting the best deal."

"Boss, the best deal is when both parties get what they want out of it, and I don't think that woman would ever settle for less than the best."

"Changing the subject, did she talk to you about shooting lessons?"

"Yes, she did. She wants to start this afternoon. First with that Smith and Wesson revolver she picked out."

"Do you think she can handle a rifle?"

"I think so. I've known lots of men that have lost arms, or parts of arms, that learn to work around their losses. She'll learn to use the part she's got left as good as fingers on a hand. I've been thinking about it. I think she'll be able to use that crook at the elbow to help her with both pistol and rifle."

By the time Ethan and Jeb had their horses separated out and in the stables, the trading was completed, and Badger Claw and Antelope, with their new Cheyenne friends, joined them at the corral to take their own horses. As the Cheyenne readied to ride out, Ethan noted that Skye's customers were departing with blankets and coats and other remnants of clothing salvaged from the renegades. Evidently, Skye had thrown in some boots, and he was glad to see they were going away with some items that would help them through the winter that was on the verge of arrival.

After the Cheyenne and their new friends left, the two men returned to the post, where they found Skye and She-Bear, with Running Fox's help, sorting through the bounty and arranging the pelts by type and quality. He noticed that another buffalo robe had joined their other, and it appeared Jeb and She-Bear had an extra robe. He began retrieving the hidden rifles and ammunition and consoled himself that the Cheyenne did not make off with much that would be useful in a battle with the army. Hopefully, the anticipated war was the product of someone's imagination anyway

Running Fox napped on top of his robe with a new deerskin tugged over his shoulders, and Ethan allowed himself a break in front of the spitting and crackling fire. He decided that the day had gone well. The main objective had been to cut the horse herd down to size, so they could take proper care of the animals. That had been accomplished, and Skye had turned the process into a capitalistic venture resulting in some merchandise with serious market value. He saw no sign of snow, and the sun had creeped out from under the smoky-looking cloud cover, so it appeared they would be underway in the morning. With their lightened load, they could make the trip back down the Powder Trail in good time.

He started at the sound of gunfire outside before he remembered that Jeb and the two women were commencing the lessons. Jeb had suggested She-Bear might have some tips for handling the rifle, and Ethan suspected Jeb wanted to evaluate her skills and decide whether he might issue a challenge for a match. Since She-Bear could shoot as well as anyone Ethan had ever seen, male or female, he doubted that such a challenge would ever be made. It might take time, but Ethan had a hunch he would not be challenging Skye to any shooting matches either.

34

ETHAN CRAWLED OUT from under the new buffalo robe early the next morning, his muscles and bones less sore because of the new robe that Skye had spread out beneath them to cushion the hard floor. He tossed a few logs on the fire and warmed his britches in front of the dancing flames before slipping them on and heading outside to take his first look at the day. When he opened the door, he was surprised to be greeted by a good foot of snow, which sent him back for his boots and sheepskin coat. Damn, the snow was still falling like goose down from the sky. They would not be saddling up and pulling out today. The big question was how soon?

After a breakfast of biscuits and venison strips, Running Fox, Ethan, and Skye trudged through the snow, leading the horses to the half-frozen stream to drink. Jeb and She-Bear headed into the woods to ferret out grazing spots that had not been covered by the snow or where the white cover could be easily brushed away. Ethan sent Running Fox to find a few solid sticks with which to break away the thin layers of ice that lined the stream's banks, while he and Skye held the horses, and he attempted to shatter the glaze with his boot heels.

"Puma, help me," the boy called, his voice choked with sobs.

Ethan and Skye both turned and stepped back from the stream bank. One Ball McLarty. He stood some fifty feet away, his left arm locked around Running Fox's neck, a blood-soaked rag covering his injured hand. His right hand gripped his favored Colt Peacemaker, with the barrel pressed to the boy's head. His shirt and fur hat were caked with snow crust, and icicles clung to his beard like a creature risen from the frozen earth.

Ethan chastised himself as a fool. How could he have let down his guard this way? He should have known that a man like McLarty was close to indestructible in these mountains. And who else would have the patience to wait nearby for his opportunity? The man was devoid of conscience. He would kill the boy in an instant if it suited him.

"It's time to deal, Ramsey," McLarty yelled in a raspy voice that betrayed his weakness. "Listen close now. I want two horses, saddled and ready to ride, brought to me right here. I expect to see some grub in the saddlebags, and bring me a decent coat while you're at it. I ain't got nothing to lose, so you don't do what I say . . . I blow the papoose's brains out."

Two horses. The son of a bitch didn't intend to ride out alone. That could not be allowed to happen. It would be a death sentence for the boy. For now, he would delay and wait for an opportunity to make a move. "Skye and I will get everything you need. Just don't hurt the boy."

"Nope, your half-breed whore ain't going no place. She's going to walk over here careful-like and trade places with the papoose. We'll stay right here till you bring the horses and supplies. And one more thing. I want a pair of saddlebags stuffed with them gold coins you and the half-breed found."

Ethan tossed a look at Skye, whose lips were set firm and whose dark eyes glared challengingly at McLarty. She handed him the reins of the two horses she had been leading and began to walk deliberately toward the mountain man.

When she reached him, McLarty released Running Fox and latched his fingers in her long hair in the same instant. He twisted her hair and yanked her near, pressing the Peacemaker barrel against her temple. "Now, get about your business," McLarty commanded. "You do what your told, the squaw will be alive when you get back."

Running Fox took the reins of Skye's horses, but his tear-filled eyes were fixed fearfully on Skye. When Ethan and the boy returned to the stable, he told Running Fox to find Jeb and She-Bear and tell them what happened and send Jeb to the stable. The boy and She-Bear should get some supplies together, the biggest coat they could scare up, a few robes and, of course, the saddle bags with gold. Ethan would bring the horses up to the trading post to pack. He decided that, to appear cooperative, he should provide a packhorse for most of the gear, but he did not intend to allow any of the animals or people to leave the trading post grounds.

Jeb showed up about the time Ethan finished saddling Razorback and a husky, sorrel gelding, which he suspected might have been Captain Quint's mount. The former soldier's dark eyes searched his own.

"The old bastard's immortal. You can't kill him," Jeb said.

"He can be killed, and the sooner, the better."

"What're we going to do boss? Do you think he'd really pull out in this snow?"

"The snow's letting up some. These early snows high up tend to hit quick and disappear for a spell before they settle in for the winter. I think he's got that figured out. That means we need to beat the hell out, too, if we don't want to spend the winter up here. Anyway, we're going to get the horses packed up. Then we'll tell Running Fox he's got to stay inside till we say he can come out."

"What do you want me to do?"

"I think you've got to stay back for now. If they leave on the horses, Skye will be separated from him. You and She-Bear be ready to take him down with your rifles. The problem is we don't know where he'll head. He's not going to take the trail we came in on. It would be too easy to follow him. He'll probably disappear into the woods as soon as he can, and then it will be hell to catch up. I'm hoping to get an opening before they get to that point."

"Boss, the man's a lunatic. And you can't trust anything he says."

"I know. And that's the reason I can't let Skye leave with him. I'll never see her alive if they ride out of here together."

35

SKYE'S HEAD WAS locked tightly against McLarty's chest, as his arm gripped her neck to him like a vice. The blood from his mutilated hand dripped on her neck. He remained unbelievably strong, but he was breathing heavily, and his rancid breath struck her face like blasts from a bellows. Of course, it had never been Running Fox he wanted. He was no doubt determined to make her pay for the damage she had inflicted, and she shuddered to think of her fate if he escaped with her as his hostage.

She tried to work the buttons of her bulky coat free, hoping she might inch her fingers into a gap and free her pistol. There was no way she could aim the pistol at a vital organ cinched against him like she was, but a foot or a knee was possible. It evidently had not occurred to McLarty that she might be armed. That fact wasn't helping her now, but, if she didn't panic, she might have her chance, and she vowed she would not hesitate to grab it. She remembered Jeb's words about handling a firearm. "Be patient, be calm, be ready."

What worried her most was Ethan. She knew he would comply with McLarty's instructions. He was doubtless formulating a plan, but the wily McLarty would know he dared not depart with Ethan alive. Ethan had been an Army Chief of Scouts, and he was no amateur as a tracker. He would follow and eventually catch up to them at some moment when the odds had changed. No, McLarty had to deal with Ethan now.

It seemed like they waited for hours in place, McLarty's body stiff and tense, his arm never relaxing its grip on her neck, his head turning repeatedly like a bird dog sniffing out game. And then Ethan appeared over the ridge on which the building site was situated. He was leading Razorback and Quint's sorrel with a packhorse trailing behind. As he approached, she willed him to stop. And he did, some twenty yards away.

"Bring me the horses, Ramsey."

"Turn her loose first."

"Don't be an ass, Ramsey. Why do you think I wanted two saddled horses?"

"I figured you wanted a switcher."

"You're not that dumb. Now bring me the horses. If you don't, I'd just as well put a bullet in her brain and be done with the whore. It would be her due for what she done to me." She could feel the cold iron of the Peacemaker barrel pressing more firmly against her temple, and she closed her eyes waiting for the blast that would send her into oblivion. "Now, bring me the horses, and then open the saddle bags, so I can see the gold."

Ethan approached slowly, and Skye knew he was thinking, searching for the right moment. She decided that when Ethan handed the reins to McLarty they would have their moment. McLarty would have to take the reins with the gun in his hand or he would have to release her. She would go limp if he did not let her loose, and her dead weight would throw the mountain man off balance, and Ethan could make a move. He was not a gunfighter, but he was quick as lightening in his reactions. He would do something. If he did release her, she would have her own pistol in hand in seconds.

As Ethan came within nearly ten feet of McLarty and Skye, McLarty croaked, "Stop right there."

Ethan obeyed.

"Open the saddle bags on the pack horse. Show me the gold."

Ethan said, "I can't do that and hold the reins of the others. You'll have to take them."

McLarty turned the Peacemaker away from Skye and pointed it at Ethan and squeezed the trigger twice. Deafening thunder roared in Skye's ears, and she was frozen with horror for a moment as she saw Ethan sink to his knees, scarlet trickling through two holes in his coat. McLarty threw her on the ground and holstered his pistol as he moved to grab the horses' reins. "Stay put, bitch, or you'll get the same."

As she tumbled to the ground cushioned by the thick blanket of snow, she released one more button of her coat and slipped her hand through the opening and pulled the pistol from its holster. She saw that McLarty was struggling with the frightened horses, trying to calm them as he tried to get to the saddlebags on the pack horse, momentarily obsessed with his potential riches. She clambered up and put her weight on one knee, raised her crippled left arm, and rested the pistol in the crook. She took her time, taking a deep breath and putting everything out of her mind but the target. The pistol held steady, and she squeezed the trigger, flinching at the gun's kick and crack. She did not see the wound between McLarty's shoulder blades, but she saw him topple backwards, landing face up on the white ground.

She got up and rushed first to McLarty. He was still alive, staring up at her in disbelief. She placed another shot between his eyes for good measure. Her task completed, she whirled and moved Ethan who lay crumpled in the snow. She thought, at first he was dead, and she found herself engulfed by unquenchable sorrow and emptiness. But, then, he coughed.

36

JEB AND SHE-BEAR eased an unconscious Ethan onto the buffalo robe Skye had spread out in front of the fireplace. Jeb and She-Bear had rushed to the gunfire and had arrived at the scene of the shooting just as Skye fired her second shot. She-Bear and Skye had removed Ethan's coat and found three wounds, one in the right rib area where a bullet had appeared to enter his side. They surmised that the second wound, located in the lower back, was caused by the exit furrowed by the bullet from the first. The other had torn a gaping hole in his chest and had been pumping blood that portended a dire end. The two women had temporarily staunched the bleeding before Jeb, with She-Bear's help, carried him to the trading post.

Knowing She-Bear had unusual skills in tribal medicine, especially for one so young, Skye deferred to her judgment in treatment of the wounds. Jeb had been a battle-hardened soldier, and when he knelt beside Ethan, the grim look on his face conveyed his pessimistic outlook.

Jeb got up and said, "I'll gather up the horses and leave Ethan's care to the two of you." He turned to Running Fox, who stood, seemingly frozen in place, near Ethan, looking on in horror. "Fox, you come help me with the horses. It won't take long if you'll help."

"Me no want to leave Puma," he said with a tremor in his voice.

"Right now, we all need to help. This is how you can help."

Jeb headed toward the door, and the boy followed, his reluctance obvious.

She-Bear had placed a small kettle of water on the fire and instructed Skye to cut away Ethan's shirt and then to find the cleanest fabric she could from any source and slice it or rip it into strips.

The fabric was no problem with the clothing they had salvaged from the renegades. Clean cloth was a challenge, though, and Skye had to make do with the least dirty. When she carried an armload of the crude bandages to She-Bear, she found her friend busy washing the area around the wounds.

She-Bear said, "The bleeding has slowed from the rib wounds. They do not seem serious . . . unless they putrefy . . . and that can happen with the slightest wound. I have some dried herbs we can boil and make us a paste much like the one I put on your face. We will apply it to your wounds again, also, although they seem to be healing nicely."

Skye had almost forgotten her own injuries, and she ran her fingers over the scabbed lesions that marked her cheek. She must be uglier than a wild pig, she thought, with the bruised eye and the scarred face. It was amazing Ethan would even look at her, let alone share her robe. What was she thinking of? What did it matter? He could send her away if he wished. She just wanted him to live. Regrets poured over her now, realizing that her dreams of just a few hours previous were fragile, as all dreams are, subject to the whims of fate. If she had only not pushed him away before she returned to Lame Buffalo's village, none of this would have happened. She would have married him, and they would now be living in peace on his ranch. Her people would not have been so needlessly slaughtered. It was strange how the seemingly insignificant decision of one person could innocently trigger a chain of events that would affect the lives of many. She supposed this happened to every person, perhaps, even daily. It was something one could think about too much.

"Sky-in-the-Morning?" It was She-Bear.

"I am sorry. I was thinking."

"Think about this. I do not know what to do about the chest wound. It is deep. I do not think I can remove the bullet. I am afraid I might do great harm if I try."

"He will die if we do not."

"Yes." She-Bear looked up at her with tear-filled eyes. "I am sorry to say this, but I fear he is near death. It is in the hands of the Great Spirit."

She-Bear's words angered her. "How can you say that? He is not going to die. He cannot do this to me. I will not allow it."

She-Bear got up. "I will prepare the poultice."

Skye sat down on the robe beside Ethan and took his hand in hers. She studied his pale face, covered by the scraggly beginnings of a beard she was not fond of. She watched his chest rise and fall. His breathing was steady and did not seem labored. She told herself this was a good sign. She spoke softly in a near whisper. "You are not going to die on me, you son-of-a-bitch. You do not dare. I will make you regret it. Do you understand?"

Ethan moaned and his lips moved. She convinced herself he was affirming he understood.

Soon, She-Bear returned and poured some of the boiling water in a tin pan and began adding various powders until she produced a yellow paste. She moved to Skye and lowered herself to her knees and began coating her injured cheek with the hot poultice. Then she applied the concoction to a small area above the eye. "Now," she said, "I will put this on your warrior's wounds. I will need you to help me with the wrapping."

"He spoke to me, you know."

She-Bear looked at Skye doubtfully. "I did not hear him."

"He spoke softly. You had to be close to him. But he spoke."

"That is good."

Skye could tell that her friend did not believe her, but it didn't matter.

Later, Jeb and Running Fox returned. "How is he?" Jeb asked.

She-Bear shook her head doubtfully. "Sky-in-the-Morning says he spoke. His breathing is steady. He would survive the wounds near his ribs. I do not have the skill to remove the bullet from his chest. It is buried in a place I would not dare touch."

Running Fox stepped quietly over to his wounded friend and sat down next to Skye. "Me afraid," he said.

"Puma like my father. Him good to me. Helps when mother die."

"Be brave, Fox. We will make him live."

Jeb said, "The snow has about stopped."

"That is good. Because we're leaving in the morning . . . at daylight. Can you make a travois?"

"Yeah, but Boss is in no shape to travel."

"Do you think he will be ready in two days . . . a week? Tell me."

"I don't know, ma'am. I don't know."

"You think he is going to die here, don't you?" She did not give him time to respond. "Well, start thinking differently. We are taking him to Dr. Henry Weintraub in Lockwood. I was supposed to die once, too." She lifted her damaged arm. "I ended up with this, but Ethan would not let me die. Now it is time for me to pay him back. Jeb, how long will it take us to get to Lockwood?"

"I don't know, ma'am. It took us more than a week to get here, but we made some long stopovers. Depends on what the snow has done to the trails. We have the advantage of downhill most of the way. I think we could do it in five, if we're lucky."

"Think three."

Jeb rolled his eyes but remained silent. "I'd better get started on the travois." He turned and walked back outside.

As nightfall cast its dark blanket over the mountains, Skye took a break from Ethan's side and tugged on her coat and the high-legginged moccasins she had taken from the dead Pawnee and walked out into the snow. She paced nervously in front of the trading post, from time to time kicking up puffs of powdery snow in frustration. The anemic wind that had come with the snow had died and left utter stillness behind, and the star-spangled sky signaled the storm had passed—for the moment anyway.

Suddenly, she stopped, and a chill raced down her spine. She could have sworn she heard the mournful howl of a coyote in the distance. She froze in place and listened. It came again, clearly now, and was followed by excited barking from a pack. Did coyotes live this high up? It would more likely be wolves, she thought. She had spent only summers with Lame Buffalo's band, and a Cheyenne city girl did not develop the keen sense of sounds that most Sioux had. But she would swear the howl was a coyote's. The Sioux within her sought meaning in this moment. Then she panicked. Had Ethan died? She whirled and raced to the cabin and barged through the door, slamming it roughly behind her before she hurried quickly to his side. She slipped her hand under the robe and placed her fingers lightly on his chest, breathless as she waited for the rhythm of his breathing. Then she felt it, and tears trickled down her cheeks. He was alive. She poked another log into the fireplace, and then she removed her coat and moccasins and crawled under the thick robe to snuggle as close as she dared to the man she loved.

37

SKYE HAD EXPERIENCED brief moments of encouragement during her nearly sleepless night. Twice Ethan had awakened, tossing and groaning, and talking unintelligible nonsense about his cattle and his horse, Patch. But both times he had also repeated her name softly and tenderly, as though summoning her to his side. She had assured him she was there and taken his hand in hers, and he had quickly faded away. At the time she did not know if he was in a coma or only sleeping, but she knew he was alive, and that was all that mattered.

This morning they had packed and saddled early. Jeb had constructed a sturdy travois with long lashed poles that were hitched to Patch's empty saddle and again by a pair of ropes that anchored around the gelding's powerful neck and shoulders. The travois bed was covered with stretched deer skins, and after they had placed Ethan on the contraption, they wrapped him like a mummy in one of the buffalo robes and tied him to the dragging stretcher to stabilize his body and to cushion him as much as possible from aggravation of his wounds as they bounced over the rugged, rocky terrain.

They were taking a brief break now, having made the crossing to the east side of the Powder River. Maneuvering the travois above the water had been the biggest challenge, but Jeb had foreseen the problem and had cut chinks in the base of the stretcher and attached a rope to the ground end of the travois poles. He wrapped it around his own broad shoulders and hoisted the end as he mounted his own horse so that Ethan was suspended above the water as he followed Patch, led by Skye mounted on Razorback. Skye was quickly realizing that Jebediah Oaks was a man of exceptional skill and resourcefulness. He never said much, but when he spoke, it made sense to listen to what he had to say. He had insisted on the stop, so he and She-Bear could take a few old blankets and dry the legs and undersides of the horses before they moved on. "We've got to take care of the animals," he said. "We don't get out of these mountains without them."

Jeb had suggested she focus on trying to get Ethan to take some water, and she was coaxing him now, with a feeling of hopelessness, carrying on a one-sided conversation with him as though he understood every word and was participating in the dialogue. She knew that he could survive the trip down the mountain without food, but water was another matter. Three or more days without water, especially with his blood loss, would make the journey to the surgeon in vain.

"You listen to me, Ethan. You are going to drink this very slowly. There is no choice. You have to, and I am going to be very angry if you do not."

She pressed the battered military canteen to his lips, thinking that her missing hand would be helpful at this moment. He mumbled something that she chose to believe was "yes, ma'am," and his dry lips sucked at the water, but he took it too fast and began to choke and cough. At least he showed signs of life. She had an idea and plucked an old kerchief she had pilfered from the renegades' things. She could not vouch for its cleanliness but decided that was the least of their worries right now, and she stuffed the end of the cloth in the canteen and, after drenching it, pressed it between Ethan's lips. He began sucking like a baby at his mother's breast. She repeated this numerous times before their departure and was satisfied he was taking in some water. It was a painstakingly slow process, and she worried whether he was getting enough.

It seemed to Skye they were crawling like snails down the mountain trail, but several hours after sunset of the first day they reached the campsite where she and She-Bear had been held at the time of their escape. She was pleased to confirm that, indeed, the backtracking trip was moving nearly twice as fast as the climb. But not fast enough. It helped that the snow was turning to a light frosting on the ground as they moved away from the high country. She wanted to travel through the night, but Jeb took command.

"You'll kill the horses, ma'am. We've got to give them time to graze and rest, and a warm fire would do us all good. I can make some biscuits, and She-Bear will get some venison strips roasting. You and Fox can tend to the boss. I don't think he's taking enough water."

"I've got an idea, and if it works, Running Fox can probably be of more help with Ethan," Skye said.

After unhitching the travois and carrying the Ethan-laden platform to the fire, the riders staked out the horses. Then Skye and Running Fox sat next to Ethan in the firelight, and Skye pulled her skinning knife from her belt and sliced off a small piece of doeskin that lapped over the travois pole. She trimmed it into a crude circular shape and punched a tiny hole in the center. Skye reached for the canteen and plucked a skinny leather thong from her pocket and began to tie the doeskin to the canteen opening.

"Me see," Running Fox said. "Make mama's tit for Puma. Feed him like papoose."

Skye noticed that the boy was grinning for the first time in several days, and she smiled back. "We'll try it now and see if it works. If it does, you can help give him water. He must have water."

"Me want to help Puma."

Skye scooted next to Ethan and instructed Running Fox to find some furs to stuff under Ethan's head, and when the boy returned, they raised Ethan's head enough to allow him to drink. Skye pressed the doeskin nipple between his lips, and he began to suckle eagerly. She nodded to Running Fox. "Can you hold this? You must be careful not to let the water go too fast into his mouth."

"Me can do this."

Skye watched as the boy carefully administered the water. His instincts were good, and he quickly had the knack for the job. And he seemed to be hugely pleased for the opportunity to help his friend.

She loosened the ropes that bound Ethan to the travois to give him some freedom of movement in the unlikely event he needed it during the night and later spread her robe on the ground next to him. She was a little surprised when Running Fox put his own robe down next to hers before he burrowed into it. She wondered if the boy was unknowingly trying to fashion a new family.

38

THEY WERE BACK on the Powder River Trail before sunrise, but after several hours on the trail an ominously dim light began to sift over the mountain tops. The dark clouds that blocked the sun's rays looked too much like those she had seen a few days back. She hoped the snow would stay higher up this time, too.

She-Bear edged her gelding past Skye and Razorback and moved ahead on the trail. Instinctively, Skye knew this was not a whimsical move, and she heightened her alertness. She looked over her shoulder and saw that Running Fox was leading She-Bear's pack horses and that Jeb was signaling a halt. She reined in Razorback and dismounted and hurried to check on Ethan. Running Fox soon joined her with the nipple-topped canteen. He drank thirstily from the canteen, but when her fingers caressed his forehead, she found the flesh burning like a raging fire. She had expected this development but hoped they could keep the fever at bay for some time yet. Perhaps She-Bear would have something among her herbs that would help.

Soon She-Bear returned, accompanied by a young mounted brave wearing buckskins, his braided hair adorned with two feathers. A wave of relief swept over her when she recognized the visitor. It was Bear Killer, a youth just short of seventeen years of age and the son of Lame Buffalo and brother of Otter. He also happened to be her cousin since her mother, Singing Lark, had been Lame Buffalo's sister.

He was the reason she had met Ethan. She had retained Ethan to represent the boy after he escaped a lynching where two of his friends had been brutally hanged for the murders of a man and a woman. While she and Ethan had ferreted out the real killers, Skye incurred the broken bone that cost her part of her lower arm. Bear Killer had been on the hunt with the other braves and warriors when the renegades attacked the village.

She rushed out to meet her cousin who raised his hand. "Greetings, my cousin," he said. "After many days of sadness, it lifts my heart to find you well." The young man, at his father's insistence, had lived four winters at the Quaker school, and Skye had taught him for two of those. He was a natural scholar and spoke English without an accent. Certainly his English was better than her Lakota.

"I am happy to see you, Bear Killer. You were not expected."

Two other young braves rode cautiously up behind Bear Killer. They were solemn-faced and obviously wary, and Skye recognized them as members of Lame Buffalo's band, although she could not recall their names. Bear Killer was a tall, sinewy, muscled young man, and his companions represented marked contrasts.

Bear Killer nodded at a short, unusually pudgy brave for a Sioux. "This is my friend, Walking Turtle." Then gesturing to the skinny, taller rider, whose ribs were outlined on his torso, he said, "This is my friend, Hungry Wolf. When the coyote told me I must find you, my friends asked to join me on the quest."

'The coyote?"

"Yes, when the hunting party returned to the village to find our people gone, Badger Claw left with others to follow your trail. The younger braves and warriors sought the location of our tribesmen, to take them the small offerings from the hunt, and found the survivors at the Puma's ranch. Otter told me the story of the brutal slaughter that took place at our village and of the death of my father. Sleep would not come that night until I heard the coyote calling to his mate in the hills. It made me think of my father's vision on the night of the coyote and gave me peace. I returned to my robe and fell quickly to sleep. It was then that the coyote visited and spoke. He said the Puma was near death and that I should find you. He said the future of our band demanded that I find you both, for the strength of the two carries big medicine."

"You have found me, and I am glad you and your friends have come. We need your help. The Puma is gravely wounded and, yes, near death. We must get him to Lockwood and the surgeon there as quickly as possible."

Bear Killer turned toward his friends and spoke in Lakota. She understood the language of her mother's people well enough. Bear Killer was explaining that their help was needed and they were engaging in animated conversation about an alternate trail. Walking Turtle and Hungry Wolf turned their ponies and headed back down the Powder River Trail.

"She-Bear has already told me of the urgency of your journey to the white medicine man. She said that the Puma is now your man. As you know, he is my friend,

and I owe him my life. I will try to repay. There is another trail that will save many hours on your return to
Lockwood. It is narrow and partially grown over, but my
friends and I will ride ahead and clear the way to ease
passage of the travois."

"Thank you, cousin. We shall follow your trail."

When she returned to Ethan's side, she found She-
Bear pouring some powders into the canteen. "These will
sometimes lower the fires," the tall woman said, re-tying
the nipple to the canteen's mouth and handing it back to
Running Fox, who pressed it between Ethan's lips.

As they readied to move forward, huge flakes of snow
began to fall from the sky.

39

AFTER RIDING, AND often walking, most of the previous night and all day, the party arrived in front of Dr. Henry Weintraub's office and hospital shortly after sundown. Skye hammered demandingly on the door until Weintraub appeared. At first his eyes widened, and the young Jewish physician seemed startled and perplexed by what might have looked like a Sioux war party outside his office. Then he recognized Skye.

"Miss dePaul?"

"Yes, Doctor. It's Ethan . . . he's been shot. Over three days ago now. You've got to save him."

Weintraub sprang into action. The tall, gangly physician called back into his office, which was a part of a large two-story home where he and his wife, Ruth, resided and also maintained a three-bed hospital. "Ruth, would you prepare the surgery? We have a badly wounded man out here."

Then Weintraub gently moved Skye aside and rushed out onto the snow-frosted street and knelt by the travois. "Untie the robe," he said to no one in particular. Jeb began uncinching the bonds while the physician felt Ethan's forehead and probed his neck for a pulse. The robe pulled back, he traced his fingers down Ethan's chest and torso. Skye watched closely, and the grim set of Weintraub's face confirmed what she already knew.

"Get this contraption into the house," Weintraub said, "and follow me to my surgery."

"Go ahead, Doctor," Skye said, "I know the way."

"Yes, I guess you would. I'll get everything prepared."

Jeb and Bear Killer, with the help of Walking Turtle and Hungry Wolf on the sides, maneuvered the travois into the physician's surgery where under Weintraub's supervision they gently lifted Ethan upon a long, sheet-covered table. Dr. Weintraub and his assistant, who happened to be his obviously pregnant wife, Ruth, started removing Ethan's clothes as Skye began to follow Jeb and the young Sioux braves from the room.

"I will return in a few moments," Skye told the physician.

"You had better find a chair in the waiting room. This will take a while."

"I am sorry, Doctor. I must be here. We are stronger together."

Weintraub tossed her a quizzical look and evidently decided he didn't have time for a losing argument. "Well, you can't wear those filthy rags in here. There are some surgical gowns in the closet just outside the door. Use one, and while you're out there put a few more logs on the fire."

When she went into the waiting room, she found Running Fox sitting on a straight-back chair. "Me stay?"

She thought a moment. "Yes, but you must wait here. Do you understand?"

"Yes. Me stay here."

She spoke briefly to Jeb. "I am sure you and She-Bear can leave the horses at Enos Fletcher's and rent some others. Tell him that the Lazy R will take care of the bill. Could you secure the furs and gold at Ethan's house? You and She-Bear can stay there for now."

"Ma'am, I don't know. Are you sure the boss would be okay with that?"

"Absolutely. Somebody needs to be there to protect the gold."

"Ma'am, there's something else you need to know about."

"What is that?"

"When we were coming down that mountain, Bear Killer told me something that's a personal worry to me and going to be a concern to all of us. He said all Sioux have been ordered to the reservation up in South Dakota by January 31, 1877. Any that don't show up will be arrested and taken there by the army. Mostly they want the Indians out of the Black Hills, but they're concerned about trouble they think Sitting Bull and his friends are stirring up in north Wyoming and southern Montana."

"That is probably where Badger Claw and his Cheyenne friends were going."

"I'd say that's likely."

"We have something over three months. I will think about this. But right this moment there is something more important on my mind."

After giving Running Fox a hug in the waiting room, Skye found a hospital gown and stripped off her filthy trail clothes, becoming aware for the first time how much she stank and needed a good bath. She was surprised that Ethan had been willing to share a robe with her. Of course, she guessed he didn't smell like a bouquet of roses, either, but she had not noticed.

She quietly entered the surgery. Dr. Weintraub was bent over Ethan, who had a cloth tossed over his lower extremities and private areas but was otherwise naked. She was instantly struck by the sight of his body's ghostly paleness. The physician was cleaning and examining the wounds.

"You did well with the rib wounds," he commented. "I'll do some flushing, but I won't suture. It's best to bandage and let it drain. The chest hole is another matter. Frankly, I don't see how he's lived this long. I just don't know how much good I can do. I want you to be prepared for the worst."

"He is not going to die. He is not allowed to do this to me." She saw the physician look doubtfully at his wife and shrug.

"The chest wound is certainly the biggest challenge I've faced as far as gunshots are concerned. The problem is the bullet is buried deep and it is located near the heart and lung and vital arteries. I can't just 'dig it out,' as the old timers say. Hippocrates said that 'first physicians should do no harm.' In all likelihood, that is exactly what I would do if I tore in there with a scalpel."

"So what are you going to do?"

"We must keep him absolutely still. If you wish, you may hold his hand. Perhaps it will calm him some. And, if not, I suspect you may find it helpful."

He had read her mind. But why should she be surprised. She already knew him to be an exceptionally insightful man. "Thank you," she replied softly, moving to Ethan's side and taking his hand in hers.

"Now," Weintraub said, "Ruth is going to administer a light dose of chloroform. He is obviously unconscious, but I can't risk his awakening or moving when I invade the wound. Then I am going to enter the wound with a Nelaton probe, which has a small porcelain nob on the end. If I think I have found the bullet, I will withdraw it, and it should show a lead mark on the end. It assures I am not misled by a bone fragment. After that, I will insert a bullet extractor that I think is appropriate to this situation. I have only used it on one other occasion, but the head screws into the bullet and I then removes the bullet with minimal damage to surrounding tissue and organs. Then I will use my forceps to remove any cloth or other foreign objects I might find from the bullet's channel."

"You make this sound so simple."

"It will take us two hours at minimum to do all of this."

40

FOLLOWING THE SURGERY, Skye, Mrs. Weintraub, and Dr. Weintraub pushed the wooden surgery table on its metal rollers into the hospital section of the facilities, and the three of them had gently let Ethan down into a single bed. The hospital was housed in a former parlor and had three beds separated by clean feed sack curtains. Skye was glad to find there were no other current occupants. She noted that changes had been made since her hospitalization, when several guest rooms had been used for patient quarters. She supposed the doctor was adapting the residence to an expanding family.

The next morning, Ethan remained unconscious, which the doctor assured her was not necessarily a bad thing for another half day or so. But he needed nourishment, something beyond the limited water he was accepting. Skye sat next to the bed, her hand holding Ethan's, Running Fox sitting beside her on another chair, sleeping with his head in her lap.

Ruth Weintraub came in and asked, "May I join you?"

"Of course, please do. Would you like my chair?"

"No. Stay put. I'll get one." She went behind the curtain and slid another across the oak floor and placed it near the foot of the bed and sat down.

Skye noticed that the young woman, probably in her mid-twenties, seemed always well-kempt and impeccably dressed. Assisting in the surgery, she seemed confident and poised even as splotches of blood began to cover her surgical apron. The sable-haired woman was incredibly beautiful, and Skye wondered how Henry Weintraub, with his perpetual mussed-up look and somewhat awkward social skills, ever won the heart of this mountain princess. Ruth, though, she remembered, was sort of a mail order bride, and their courtship had been carried on by correspondence

"Your husband was impressive during the surgery. He gave me great confidence."

"He's very skilled. And very smart. He was a brilliant surgeon in a Philadelphia hospital. I'm a little embarrassed. I met him by way of a notice he posted in a medical journal seeking a woman who would be willing to correspond. I am a trained nurse, and I was working at the same hospital Henry once served. That was a half dozen years before my time there. The people who remembered him thought he was a god. He wrote persuasive letters," she smiled broadly. "But he warned me that he wanted to remain in the West and would never have any money. Fortunately, I got caught up in his dream. We met for the first time when he met my train in Cheyenne and were married two hours later." She patted her bulging belly. "Anyway, here we are, and here we'll raise our family."

"You seem to be a good team."

"I think so. I understood when you said you and Ethan were stronger together. Now you are going to leave Ethan for a time. I have filled our one luxury, a claw-footed bathtub, with hot water. It's in the room off the kitchen . . . and you can enjoy a bath. You will find a bar of lye soap and perfumes on the shelf. I've taken the liberty of laying out some of my things for you to wear. We seem to be about the same size . . . when I'm not carrying a boulder in my belly. When you finish, we'll see what we can do for the boy. For now, we can put him in one of the hospital beds.

As evening approached, Skye, savoring the feel of freshness that came after her bath, noticed that Ethan was starting to shift on his bed and blinked his eyes from time to time. "A good sign," Weintraub confirmed.

Ruth Weintraub had made a quick trip to the general store to purchase a few shirts, a pair of denim britches and some underthings for Running Fox, and, Skye, over the boy's protests, had administered a bath and stood by while he squirmed into the new clothes.

"Me no want to be white boy," Running Fox protested.

"You're not a white boy," Skye countered. "You are a young Sioux brave dressed in a white boy's clothes. You will always be a Lakota, but you must learn to live in the white man's world."

"Me want to live with Lakota."

"You do not want to live with the Puma?"

"Me want him to live with my people."

Skye left the argument at that. She had more important matters to consider and decisions to make. First, when—not if—Ethan recovered, would they marry? It was one thing to talk marriage far removed from civilization and the practicalities of everyday life, but perspective had a way of changing things. Did she really want to bind herself to sharing her life with a man and the compromises that it would inevitably entail? She and Ethan must talk, and, perhaps, they should not rush this change in their lives.

Then there was the matter of Running Fox. The boy had attached himself to Ethan, who was as close to a parent as the boy now had. She must talk seriously with Ethan about the future of the boy.

The government's reservation order. She, of course, was half-white and had been raised primarily in Cheyenne and would presumably be exempted from any order, and there would no doubt be other exemptions. She would rely upon Ethan to untangle the legal technicalities. She feared the outcome of reservation life for those she still thought of as her people. She knew that the reservation experience had not been positive for other tribes and those of the Lakota who had travelled the reservation road before. In many instances, it led to lives of dependency, deprivation, and starvation. Many, perhaps well-intentioned, bureaucrats were simply incompetent when it came to managing the lives of other people. And she thought that too many of those who were competent were dishonest and diverted government funds to unscrupulous contractors. She, at least, wished for the survivors of her village to have a choice other than the reservation. But was that possible?

This took her to the gold. She was in possession of considerable wealth, but was it hers to dispose of as she wished? She had never thought of it as truly hers. She knew her father had been something of a rogue—but a lovable one from her viewpoint. He had doubtless swindled the Cheyenne out of the gold for a few dollars in trade goods. And there was the matter that the gold had been stolen from the United States government in the first place. Ethan had already suggested on several occasions that the United States government might have a legal claim for the money and that there would be an obligation to notify the army of the discovery. Whether the government had a valid claim or not, she could not imagine that it would not be pursued and eventually recovered. She had no qualms about keeping the gold and setting it aside for the use of her people. She easily rationalized that this would be a partial payment for the lands the whites had confiscated. It occurred to her that this had the potential of being a huge conflict between her and Ethan. Should this be resolved before any further talk of marriage?

Skye dePaul did not dwell easily in a world in limbo. She had always been a decision-maker. Now she had to decide.

41

I T WAS PAST midnight, and Skye lay awake on one of
Dr. Weintraub's hospital beds that had been shoved
against Ethan's so she was within easy reach and
sight. Running Fox slept on the remaining bed curtained
off on the other side of her. She had made her decisions
but, now, how to carry them out and make them happen
was the challenge. Nothing mattered, though, until she
was assured Ethan was truly on his way to recovery.

Henry Weintraub had been noticeably agitated when
Skye had announced after supper that she would be
sleeping next to Ethan tonight. "There is nothing you can
do," he said, "and you are not married. It would be a bit
improper, don't you think?"

But Ruth, who was quickly becoming her friend and
ally, interceded. "Henry, don't be so straitlaced. Someone needs to be with the patient. I'm not going to sit up

all night with him, and it seems foolish for you to do so when you have someone who has seen the man through this from the beginning to keep watch."

In the end, Dr. Weintraub was not interested in taking on the two women and had left the room with a parting remark, "Whatever the two of you decide is okay for tonight, but I need to make my beds available for other patients tomorrow."

After he had departed the dining room, Ruth explained, "Most people are cared for at home, and the beds are only used occasionally for surgical recoveries and the like. I'll see that you remain for as long as you like."

"Thank you. And assure Henry that nothing improper will happen within the confines of his hospital." Considering Ethan's condition, this was an easy promise to keep.

Skye was troubled only a little about some of the decisions she had made. She worried she was not being as open and honest with Ethan as she should be. She admitted her devious streak, and she hoped Ethan would forgive her for it—or tolerate it. Now, if only he would wake up.

On cue, a voice beside her mumbled, "Skye, are you here?"

She scooted closer to him and took his hand. "Of course. Where else would I be?"

"Feel like I've been stomped by a herd of buffalo."

She held her hand to his face. "You look like it, too. But I love you anyway, Ethan Ramsey." She leaned over and kissed him on the cheek.

"I'm thirsty," he croaked, "and hungry."

She got up and went to the lamp table next to the opposite side of the bed and lighted the kerosene lump, dimming it so the glare would not be uncomfortable. She poured him a glass of water from a pitcher there and asked, "Can you hold a glass?"

He moved his fingers, testing their strength. "I don't think so."

"I can't hold your head up and help you drink at the same time. You've been sucking the nipple for the past four days."

"I've been what?"

"You heard me." She figured it would do him good to ponder for a while. She retrieved the pillow from her bed and layered it over his own as he lifted his head. Then she helped him drink. She pulled the glass away when she felt he had taken too much for the moment.

"Still hungry?" she asked.

"Starving."

"Dr. Weintraub said you have to start slowly. Ruth left ground corn and some molasses for a mush in the kitchen. I'll mix some with water and bring you a bowl with a slice of bread."

"Forget the mush."

"You've got to eat that before you get the bread."

42

ETHAN REMEMBERED EATING some corn mush and a slice of bread and being awakened several times by Skye to take healthy drinks of water. But mostly he must have slept. He awoke now to find Running Fox standing by his bed with a sober, concerned look on his face.

"Good morning, Fox," he said, smiling.

The boy beamed. "Puma. You wake up. You not die."

"It appears not."

"I be back. Nurse Ruth say I tell her when you wake up." The boy shot out of the room.

Soon he returned with Ruth Weintraub.

"Good morning, Ruth."

"Hello, Ethan. I'm pleased to see you looking much better. By the way, it's afternoon, nearly three o'clock, as a matter of fact. Can you eat something?"

"I could eat a cow."

"Well, I can come close. I have roast beef simmering and fried potatoes with some green beans I put up last summer. I can add a slice of fresh-baked bread. I'll bring you a small plate and you can eat what you're able."

"I would be very grateful. Where's Skye?"

"She left early this morning. I thought she might be back by now. She said she had a lot of business to take care of and some shopping to do, but she promised to be here before dark."

"Didn't take her long to abandon me . . . don't take me seriously. I doubt if she's been far away since I took the bullets."

"Glued to you would be more like it. She only left after Henry promised her you were going to be fine."

"Is Henry here?"

"No, he's at the Conner place. Emma's having her baby. He said to tell you it's all right to sit up when you feel like it. He wants you to start moving around . . . very slowly. Pay attention to your body. Do this in baby steps. Skye gave Running Fox instructions to look after you while she's gone. I don't think he'll be far away. If you need anything, just tell him, and he can find me if necessary. I'll return in a few minutes with something to eat."

He looked forward to Skye's return. He loved her more than she could know, and he missed her presence. He doubted he would ever get accustomed to any separations they endured. It also made him nervous that she was running around loose in the county, up to God knows what. He was certain life with the woman would never be dull. He worried a bit about whether she might have second thoughts about marriage. The spontaneous nature of their talk of marriage had left everything somewhat indefinite, and, in retrospect, he was not entirely confident she was serious. He hoped they could be married in the spring, or by summer anyway. He had no idea what she had in mind for a wedding, but he would pretty much go along with what she wanted. Her commitment was all he cared about. The road they took to get there didn't matter much.

When Ruth returned with his meal, it looked like a feast to Ethan, and he easily cleaned his plate. He would have eaten another serving, but Ruth told him he had to wait and give the meal time to digest. He could have a light meal in the evening, and if things went well she would put him on full feed in another day. She had a holiday meal planned for tomorrow anyway.

"Holiday? I surely didn't sleep till Christmas."

"We're going to celebrate your recovery," she had said, giving him a mischievous wink and smile.

The meal, coupled with his weakness, made him drowsy, and he dropped off to sleep for several hours. When he awakened, he felt a powerful urge to pee and asked Running Fox to pull the chamber pot out from under the bed. He was grateful to have the boy handy, so he did not require Ruth's help with the intimate task.

Skye returned after sundown and, after setting down her packages, bent over the bed and greeted him with a lingering kiss on the lips. She stepped back and her eyes took on a serious look as she seemed to be appraising him. Then they brightened, and she smiled approvingly.

"I think you'll do," she said, "but you stink. I'm going to talk to Ruth and see if we can figure out a way to get you cleaned up. I know you'll have to wear the hospital gown for a few days, but I was out at the Lazy R and picked up some clean clothes. I dropped those by while you were asleep before I went shopping for some things. We need to talk after supper."

"We can talk now."

"I need to think first." She gave him a kiss on the cheek, and she scurried away. "I'm going to speak with Ruth."

Less than a half hour later, Skye returned with a kettle of hot water and a wash basin with a towel and some cloths. Then she left again and brought back a ragged canvas tarp. "We're going to slide this under you, so we don't get the bedding wet. You'll have to help."

She directed Running Fox to get on the other side of the bed to pull the tarp through when Ethan raised up, and, after a brief struggle, they had the tarp spread beneath him. Skye sent Running Fox for a bar of lye soap and quickly helped Ethan out of his night shirt before he had a chance to protest. He lay naked on the bed as Skye started to soap him down, first washing gently around the wounds.

"It is strange," she said, "I have let you take advantage of me several times, but it was always in the dark. I had not seen you totally naked before."

He could actually feel himself blushing. "Fox could help me with this."

"No, it's time we got better acquainted, I should think. When we get through the dirt and grime, it appears you will pass inspection."

She proceeded to wash his private parts, and he felt enough life there that he tried to turn his mind to other thoughts and partially succeeded.

"Roll on your side, so I can wash your behind."

God help him. He complied, flinching at some pain in his chest when he did so.

Finally, she dried him down, more diligently than necessary, he thought, before she helped him into a new night shirt. Then she shaved him with a razor she had brought back from the ranch. "Sorry for the nicks. I guess we will have matching faces."

"Your face is healing nicely, and you are beautiful."

That earned him another kiss. She sent Running Fox to the kitchen to see if Ruth needed some help.

"Now," she said, "I have only one question. Since you have already taken my innocence from me, do you still intend to marry me?"

"Yes, of course. But I didn't exactly 'take' your innocence. As I recall, it was your idea. You more or less extended an invitation."

"But wouldn't a true gentleman have declined?"

"If so, I've never met a true gentleman."

"Well, I guess it doesn't matter, if you will make me an honest woman."

"You set the date, and I'll make you an honest woman."

"Tomorrow. Judge McMullen, the circuit judge, is in town, and he has agreed to stay over a day and come here to do whatever he has to do to make us legal. He is going to marry Jeb and She-Bear at the same time. Two o'clock tomorrow afternoon. I trust you will be there."

"I have no choice given the location."

"After we're married, I hope we can sleep bare-skinned. You look absolutely ridiculous in a night shirt."

He finally could not resist a grin. "I'll sleep any way you want, as long as we're together."

She kissed him on the lips, passionately this time. "That's going to be for the rest of our lives, Puma. And I'm planning to raise a litter of our kittens."

43

AFTER SUPPER, DR. Weintraub gave Ethan a thorough examination while Skye stood nearby. The physician's wife had taken Running Fox into the kitchen to teach him the game of checkers and thereby give Skye some time alone with Ethan.

When Weintraub was finished, he told Ethan, "You're a miracle man, Ethan. You should have been dead before you got to my office. There is very little indication of infection. No sign of the wounds putrefying. I can't explain it. Must be something this Bear woman gave you. I may have to have a word with her."

"When do I get out of here?"

"I'd like you to stay another two or three days, so I can keep an eye on things . . . and I'm concerned if you leave that you'll try to do too much and tear open the wounds."

"Am I well enough to get married?"

"I'd be afraid to say no. But, frankly, if Miss dePaul is going to stay here with you, I would be more comfortable if you were married." He nodded at Skye. "Ruth said you have some things to talk over together, so I'll turn the law wrangler over to you, ma'am"

After the physician left, Ethan turned his head expectantly to Skye. "You said we had things to talk about."

"First, the wedding. As I said, Judge McClellan will officiate. I have invited Will Bridges and his wife and Joe Hollings and Rachael Cooper, who are becoming something of a couple. Bear Killer and Otter, of course. They're my only living relatives. The Weintraubs will be hosts. I hope it is okay that I asked your secretary, Katherine. Is there anyone else you wish to invite?"

"I don't have any family, but I'd like to invite Enos Fletcher. He's an ornery cuss, but he's always got my back. And this spectacle should give him something to talk about the rest of his days. With that in mind, do you think you can persuade She-Bear to keep her scalps at home?"

"Jeb has already spoken with her about that."

"I will speak to Mr. Fletcher in the morning. Ruth and I will be working on a cake and refreshments when you and I are finished here. Next item."

"We have an agenda?"

"Of sorts. Running Fox is next."

"What about him?"

"Would you be willing to adopt him?"

Ethan knew the boy was something he would have to deal with at some point. Could he just send him away? It would break the boy's heart—his own as well.

"That's a decision we both have to agree upon, but, of course, I would be willing."

"Done. I guess the lawyer can work out the details. We have ourselves a son."

"Is that all?"

"No. While you were unconscious, we learned that all Sioux have been ordered to the reservation by January 31st. I do not want Lame Buffalo's band to go there, if they choose not. Some will likely be drawn to the security they think is there. But I want those who wish to be free to remain."

"It might be doable. I'm somewhat familiar with the laws and regulations in this area. I'd have to look at the recent order, but generally there are exceptions for those married to U.S. citizens . . . which, in light of Jeb's military service, should cover She-Bear. The tribes are generally treated as separate nations, but I would think Indians would be natural born citizens and entitled to the rights of any individual. The Supreme Court has not yet made that decision, though. Therefore, they are considered foreigners under the law. Anyway, proof of individual self-sufficiency is generally an exception."

"What does that mean?"

"That the Indian has a way of making his living independent of the tribe. For instance, perhaps she or he has settled in a community and offers valuable services to the public. In the end, as a practical matter, I think the government will round up those who are living in significant groups and pose a threat of waging war. I would certainly use whatever legal skills I have to keep those who do not wish to go to the reservation from going there."

"That takes me to the final matter: the gold."

"I somehow had a notion we'd end up there. I've told you, I think we should notify the military authorities. I'm not certain it's yours."

"It's not. It belongs to those who recovered it. I have given one-fourth each to Jeb and She-Bear. I am claiming one-fourth. You can give your share to the government, if you wish."

With this one, she got under his skin. "You can't do that. It's not yours to give away."

"But I already did. I suppose you could sic the government on your friends who saved your life . . . and your wife, if you still want me. Three of us have agreed to donate our shares to a worthy cause. We do not see the government as worthy. We need to find a lawyer who is smart enough to set up an organization that would take the funds and help our tribesmen become independent. It might buy land and parcel it out to those who would establish small ranches or farms . . . like the Homestead Act. After they operated the land successfully for five years, it would be deeded to them. For those who wished to establish other enterprises, the organization might make loans. The possibilities are unlimited. We would call it the 'Lame Buffalo Association.'"

"What are you doing to me?"

"You're the best lawyer in Wyoming . . . probably the whole United States. I know you could figure out how to do this."

"Oh, hell. I'm checkmated."

About the Author

Ron Schwab is the author of several Western novels, including Night of the Coyote and Last Will, nominees for Best Novel Peacemaker Awards by Western Fictioneers. He is a member of the Western Writers of America, Western Fictioneers, and Mystery Writers of America.

Ron and his wife, Bev, divide their time between their home in Fairbury, Nebraska and their cabin in the Kansas Foot Hills.

For more information, please visit his website at RonSchwabBooks.com